The Mine

Tales from a Revolution: Connecticut

Also by Lars D. H. Hedbor,
available from Brief Candle Press:

The Prize: Tales From a Revolution - Vermont
The Light: Tales From a Revolution - New-Jersey
The Smoke: Tales From a Revolution - New-York
The Declaration: Tales From a Revolution - South-Carolina
The Break: Tales From a Revolution - Nova-Scotia
The Wind: Tales From a Revolution - West-Florida
The Darkness: Tales From a Revolution - Maine
The Path: Tales From a Revolution - Rhode-Island
The Freedman: Tales From a Revolution - North-Carolina
The Tree: Tales From a Revolution - New-Hampshire
The Siege: Tales From a Revolution - Virginia
The Will: Tales From a Revolution - Pennsylvania
The Convention: Tales From a Revolution - Massachusetts
The Oath: Tales From a Revolution - Georgia
The Powder: Tales From a Revolution - Bermuda

The Mine

Lars D. H. Hedbor

Brief Candle
Press

Cover and book design: Brief Candle Press.
Cover image based on "New England Landscape," Albert Bierstadt.
Map reproduction courtesy of Library of Congress, Geography and Map Division.
Fonts: Allegheney, Doves Type, and IM FELL English.

First Brief Candle Press edition published 2020.
www.briefcandlepress.com

ISBN: 978-1-942319-37-5

Dedication

*to all men and women everywhere
who have suffered imprisonment
in the pursuit and defense of liberty*

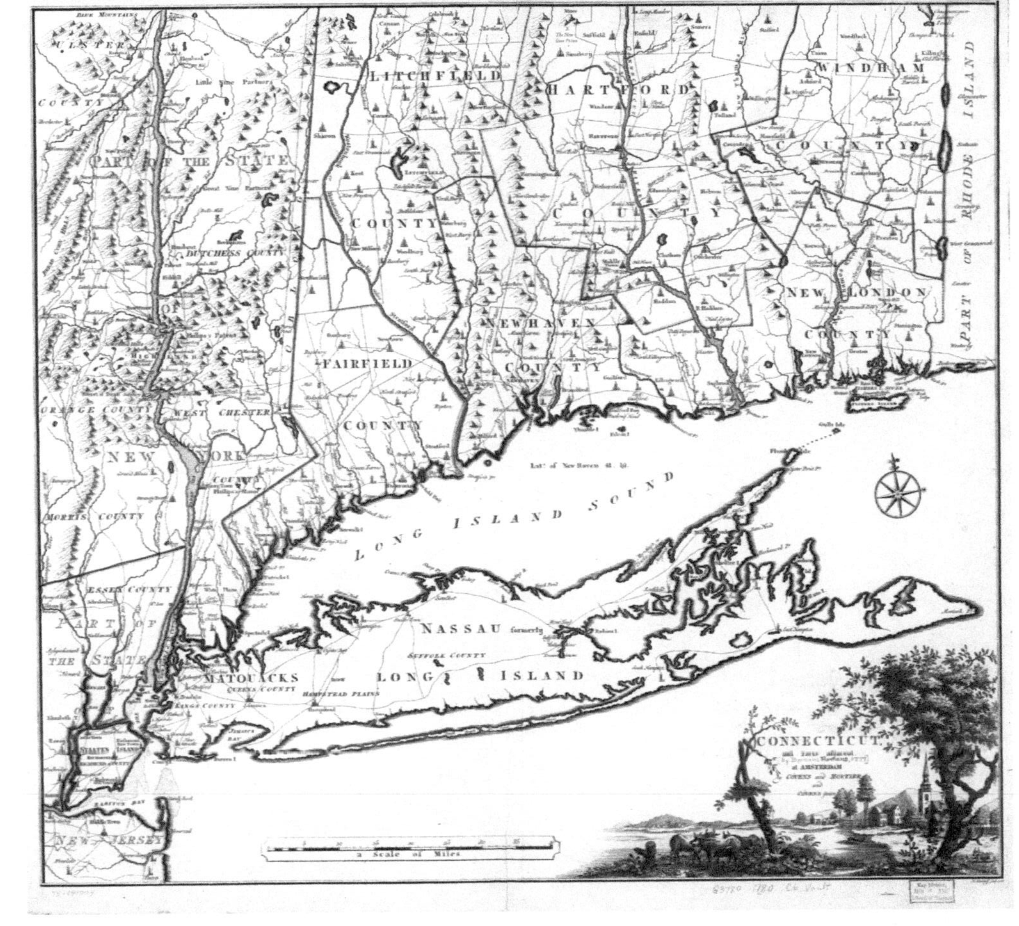

BLUE MOUNTAINS
ULSTER COUNTY
PART OF THE STATE
DUTCHESS COUNTY
LITCHFIELD
COUNTY
HARTFORD
COUNTY
WINDHAM
COUNTY
NEW LONDON
COUNTY
NEW HAVEN
COUNTY
FAIRFIELD
COUNTY
WEST CHESTER
ORANGE COUNTY
COUNTY
NEW YORK
COUNTY
MORRIS COUNTY
ESSEX COUNTY
PART OF
THE STATE
STATEN ISLAND
NEW JERSEY
RARITON BAY
AMBOY
PART OF RHODE ISLAND
Latt. of New Haven 41. 19.
LONG ISLAND SOUND
NASSAU formerly
SUFFOLK COUNTY
LONG ISLAND
MATOUACKS
QUEENS COUNTY
HEMPSTEAD PLAINS
KINGS COUNTY
a Scale of Miles
CONNECTICUT
with parts adjacent
at AMSTERDAM
COVENS and MORTIER

Chapter I

Alec Tinsworth looked up, bidding the sun farewell. He didn't know how long it would be before he saw its light again, how long he would instead live by the flickering light of torches and candles — or less.

The man at the top of the mine shaft looked down at him without pity, and Alec returned his baleful glare, his feet questing one after the other for the next step on the unsteady ladder. At last, he came to a point where there was no next step, and the guard shouted down at him, "Just drop on down. It's not so far as you will fall into the hereafter."

A coarse bark of laughter echoed down the shaft to Alec's ears, and he lowered himself by his arms alone, the chain between his manacles limiting his ability to ease down. He grimly felt for the floor that he expected to find, his foot describing wider and wider arcs through open air, until he lost his grip on the ladder and fell with a grunt in a jumbled pile of limbs. He rolled along the floor, which he was relieved to discover was strewn with straw. Without that, his fall might have done more than merely knocked his breath out for a moment.

As he lay catching his breath, he heard another guffaw from overhead, followed by the echoing boom of the door closing. The dim light that reached the bottom of the pit winked out, and Alec stayed very still, his eyes adjusting to the incredible darkness in which he now found himself.

As he waited for his eyes to find enough light to let him see his way deeper into the living quarters he'd been told to expect in the abandoned mine, he thought about the bitter road that had brought him here.

⁂

The light of the waning moon glinted through the bare branches of the woods, and Alec walked as silently as he could, desperately trying to find his way back to his patrol. He heard the snap of a twig stepped upon by a less cautious foot than his own, followed by a challenge in a low, urgent voice.

"King and country," the stranger called out, and Alec felt a wave of relief wash over him like the morning's first splash of water from a springtime stream.

He answered wearily, "King and country," and stepped out into a small clearing, where the wan light of the slender moon shone clearly on him.

The other voice called out more confidently now. "Got ourselves another Tory straggler, John."

Alec felt a different sort of chill wash over him, and the stranger now addressed him, his tone not unkind, but firm.

"If you be armed, you'd best drop down your weapon, good sir. We'll be delivering you up for parole, if you be an officer, and for prisonment otherwise."

"I've no weapon, save my knife," Alec called back resignedly.

He raised his hands where anyone could see them in the moonlight, and the stranger stepped into the clearing with him, soon followed by his companion.

The one who had to be John stepped around behind Alec, his hands questing along his prisoner's waist, and up to his raised hand, which he pulled down behind Alec's back, reaching up to bring the other beside it. "Where's this knife, friend? I don't feel a belt or bag upon you."

"Nay, I've neither. 'Tis in my boot, this one." He slowly raised his left foot, balancing carefully on the right.

"Stand steady, Tory. I'll retrieve it while Jim binds your hands."

Jim's hands took the place of John's, and Alec could feel the rough texture of hempen rope being wrapped securely around his wrists, as John pushed his raised foot to the ground and reached into Alec's boot top to retrieve the knife.

John stepped back, and Alec could see him testing the blade's edge with his thumb in the half-light. Shaking his head in disappointment, John tossed the knife off into the darkness.

"Smart of you not to run or resist, Tory." Jim's voice sounded calm in Alec's ear. "John's not afraid to shoot into the darkness when he is confident that no friendly forces lie before us."

"That knife would have done you no good against any man, either," said John. "Have you a name, Tory?"

"Aye," Alec said glumly. "I am Alexander Tinsworth, of His Majesty's Loyal Connecticut Militia, a private soldier."

Jim asked, his voice astonished, "Alec? Why, your father and mine worked together in town, before the troubles started. I'm Jim Hudgins, and my old Pa was always suggesting that I'd do well to emulate your good example, in all the things your father used to tell him about you."

He chuckled humorlessly to himself and added, "I don't

suppose that my Pa would say quite the same now, though, if he were still with us to offer an opinion."

"I am sorry to hear that you've lost your father, Jim. My dad spoke well of him, up until he turned traitor to the King."

Jim cuffed him across the face with the back of his hand, though without much conviction behind the blow. He said, "'Tis not my father who is found traitor to his country tonight, Alec. You'll keep a civil tongue in your mouth while we bring you in, and the captain will decide what's to be done with you."

John had poked Alec in the ribs then, pointing toward the first blush of sunrise visible through the trees. "You'll walk in front, Alexander, just in case there are any of your allies about, waiting to spring a trap on travelers. Don't get any ideas about running, though. We know these woods as least as well as you, and our hands aren't bound, so you'd likely just wind up tripped or tackled for your trouble. Then I'd be obliged to hobble you, though it might slow us all up even more."

His shoulders slumped, and his cheek warm from where Jim had struck him, Alec trudged into the darkness in the direction indicated. Behind him, he could hear Jim and John speaking quietly, but could only make out an occasional snatch of their conversation.

"Real shame about that family," he heard, but he didn't know if they were talking about his family or some other that had suffered misfortune in this accursed war.

His parents had most recently been turned out of the home where Alec had grown up, the home that his grandfather had built of straight timber felled from their own land. It was forfeit to the self-styled Committee of Safety, claimed as the price to be paid by a notorious Loyalist family, they'd said.

Alec's father had set his jaw in the way he always did when faced with unbearable things that could not be changed, and had gathered up the few things that the committee's representatives permitted him. Alec's mother, though, had fallen to her knees before the leader of the squad, wailing and begging that their property be spared.

The man's face had started out, resolute, and the longer Alec's mother carried on, the stormier his face became. Finally, he'd called out to Alec's father, who was still carrying armloads of his papers and clothing out to the dooryard for inspection.

"Sir, please gain control of your wife, else we shall be forced to silence her on your behalf."

Alec's father had hurried to his wife's side and bent beside her as Alec looked on, helpless rage coursing through his body. He stroked her back and spoke soothingly into her ear, and she'd regained her composure sufficiently to stand and stagger over to where Alec stood.

"See to your mother," his father had said brusquely, and had turned away, going back to the task at hand.

Alec had stood beside her, feeling her quake with silenced sobs as she clutched his arm, and had resolved in that moment to do whatever it took to ensure that she need never again suffer powerless grief.

Alec was yanked out of this reminiscence by John's question to Jim, "Think we'll find any more of these sorry fellows tonight?"

Jim's voice carried more clearly than John's in the morning air, and Alec could hear him say, "Nay, I think we've got enough to fill up the mine already, and work what may be left to work there."

That had been the first Alec had heard about the mine, and now he found himself confronted with the reality of it, whatever that might be. In the inky void beyond him, he heard men muttering to one another, and then a clear voice called out to him.

"Got you with the short ladder, too, eh?" The voice was gruff, but laced with good humor. "Can you stand, or were you hurt when you dropped?"

Alec struggled to his feet, and cursed as his head struck a low overhang. He heard a rough chuckle from the darkness.

"I guess standing upright hurt you more that falling did, eh?"

"Aye," Alec said, reaching up to feel where the ceiling was. His hand found a rough, low surface, damp with condensation. "If they mean to have men live down here, they ought make it fit for dogs, at the least."

He heard a rumble of appreciative laughter from an unknown number of men, punctuated by a new voice calling out, "Have a care what you wish for, boyo, lest our loving watchers decide that you possess the perfect means by which to accomplish it."

He could sense the nods of the men around the speaker, though he still could not see them. He asked hesitantly, "Have we no light at all down here?"

Another rumble of laughter answered him, this time less appreciative than knowing. The first man who'd addressed him answered.

"Aye, but we like to save it for when we eat. They'll give

us oil for the lamps when they want us to work, but there's been no work for days now."

Alec walked unsteadily toward the voices, his chained hands out before him to feel for obstacles. He found a wall, and felt his way along it until he bumped headlong into a human form.

"Pardon me," he muttered.

"Don't worry about it," the huddled form mumbled, and Alec could hear the muffled clink of manacles.

He had the sense that the man had turned around to face away from him. Feeling his way down the wall with his shoulders, Alec lowered himself to the floor and sat down, his own back to the rough-hewn stone.

The gruff voice called out from just in front of him, "What's your name, son?"

"I'm Alexander Tinsworth, but most folks just call me Alec."

"Thomas," the other man replied, "just Thomas. I'm the leader of the prisoners here at New-Gate, I guess you could say. Been down here since they rebuilt the place last winter. Won't say I'm happy to have you here, any more than you're happy to be here, if I don't miss my guess." A mirthless chuckle sounded in the man's throat, and died as quickly as it had started.

Alec ventured a question. "How many are we down here?"

Thomas answered, "Twenty-eight, including you, unless Robert has given up the ghost since we checked him last."

A thin, raspy voice came from a corner that somehow seemed even darker than the rest of the room. "I ain't died yet, so you'll still have to give me my ration, and not keep it for yourselves like you did Frederick's until the guards smelled him out."

Thomas' easy laugh answered the man, and he said, "Hope springs eternal, Robert. But we'll all be on short rations soon enough, if they can't find anything for us to do to earn our keep."

"Isn't this a mine?" Alec's confusion was genuine. "Not that I look to take up mining as an occupation, but it seems as though that would be a natural way to ensure that we've enough rations to spare..." His voice trailed off as Thomas began to laugh in earnest.

When the other man could speak through his chortles, he finally said, "Aye, and though the ore down here is pretty near to exhausted, you would think that, only they figured out pretty quickly that it wasn't such a good idea to put digging tools into the hands of prisoners."

Alec could almost see the flash of Thomas' grin before the man continued in a mock grumble, "We'd gotten a good start on a new tunnel to the outside, before they smoked out what we were up to." He snorted. "They only came down to inspect because they thought we had simply exhausted the vein, and wanted to see where they could have us dig out better ore than the rock we were sending up."

Alec nodded into the darkness, aware even as he did so that his interlocutor could not see his reply. "So, what manner of work have they given you since then?"

"They had us making and mending for a bit, until they figured out that we were even worse at that than we were at mining. Also, poor Jenkins had his accident with a needle and a pair of scissors."

A couple of the men broke into laughter at that, and Thomas

explained, "Jenkins had been informing on us – 'twas probably him who gave the guards the hint that we were up to more than simply mining – and he somehow wound up with the scissors halfway through his head. Not sure how he managed to sew his own mouth shut before the scissors stopped him."

After another bout of rough laughter broke out, Alec realized that they were laughing at the abuse and murder of a fellow prisoner, and he shuddered.

"In any event," Thomas said, "after that, they took away all the sharp objects. One of the guards asked me last week whether any of our number had experience with nail-making, though, so we may have a new industry before long."

"You converse with them? How?"

"Oh, they get near as bored as we do, particularly late at night. For the most part, they're decent enough fellows, just a little on the hard-edged side. Of course, so are we, I suppose." Thomas sighed. "All right, let's get a look at each other, and you can meet the other fellows, as well."

Alec was about to open his mouth to ask how, when he was nearly blinded by a long spark in the direction from which Thomas' voice had been coming. In the brief flash of light, he got the impression of a series of long tables, and men sitting on benches on either side of them. He thought he'd seen bunks against the rock wall behind them, but he couldn't be sure.

Another spark pierced the darkness, and Alec could see it find its mark in a bit of charcloth enclosed in the base of a candle holder. It flared into flame, and he thought that the man who carefully tilted a candle into it must have been Thomas.

The candle sputtered and smoked, and the light it gave was

too much at first for Alec's dark-adapted eye, but as he grew used to it, he could take in the group of men who sat peering back at him with the same curiosity that he was certain animated his own face.

Most appeared to be around his own age, though Thomas was far from the most grizzled of the bunch. None appeared to have seen a barber at any point in the recent past, and most of their faces were smudged with the gritty dirt under which they lived. A few men lounged in the bunks Alec had spotted, but most sat upright at the table, empty trenchers and a scattering of cups before them.

Whether they had just finished a meal, or sat at the table out of stubborn habit from their daylight lives, Alec could not tell.

The space was larger than Alec had originally guessed it to be, stretching away into darkness beyond the end of the tables. The ceiling was indeed low, but Alec was chagrined to note that the spot he'd bashed his head against was a timbered bracing that he could have easily ducked under, had he but known it was there.

Looking back to Thomas and catching the man's eyes, he nodded. "Good to know you, Thomas, though I do wish it were under happier circumstances."

"Same here, Alec. I'll let the rest introduce themselves before I snuff the candle, but I did want a chance to take your measure by sight, rather than solely by the sound of your voice. You're younger than I'd thought, but that's no bad thing, as it will give you more strength to draw upon in the days ahead."

He gestured to the man on his right. "Clem, go ahead and introduce yourself."

Clem was a nervous, scrawny boy, and Alec guessed he had to walk hunched over most everywhere in the mine.

The boy spoke, his voice hesitant. "Uh, I'm Clem. Got here a month and a fortnight ago, same as most of us. We was overrun by a rebel militia, and they done packed us down here to keep us out of the way."

The man beside him spoke up next, and each of the rest of the men introduced themselves in turn. Only a few stood out to Alec. One grey-haired man sat with his spine ramrod-straight, as though he were not half a hundred feet underground, and introduced himself as "Benjamin Miller, late of Fanning's King's American Regiment."

His eyes narrowed, the older man demanded, "How goes the war, young man?"

Alec frowned, unsure how to satisfy the man's evident thirst for intelligence of matters of which he himself knew little. "In truth, sir, I was separated in a fog from my company, and have been keeping low for some days now. Prior to that, I know only that we were everywhere on the move, but whether we pursued the rebels or were pursued by them, I cannot say with any certainty."

The old man's mouth screwed up in a firm grimace, and he shook his head sharply, giving the next man in turn a pointed glance.

Alec didn't think there was much chance that he'd be able to keep very many of the men's names straight, but somehow, he had little doubt that he'd be able to remember Miller without effort.

The last few men in the bunks gave their introductions, including Robert, who looked as spent as his voice had sounded. Alec could well believe that they would be sharing out his rations in a matter of days, but he kept his thoughts to himself.

Finally, they came to the man who hunched by himself

beside where Alec had taken his own seat. Thomas called out to the man after everyone had stared expectantly at him for a long moment.

"William, will you introduce yourself to the man, or will we do it for you?"

The man grunted and turned to face back toward Alec. "William," he said sourly. "They think I took George's bread last night, so they've made me stay off the furniture until I give him mine tonight." The man looked defiantly at Alec. "I didn't take it, but this lot don't care. They made up their mind even before the bread went missing, and then it was just a matter of finding some cause to pin on me."

He hunched back over himself, and turned back toward the wall.

Thomas spoke up then. "William thinks he's better than the rest of us, since he started out as a member of the King's own regiment, come here all the way from Gloucester, and he thinks that gives him the right to put on airs and take more than his share."

Alec knew the type; he'd served with a few such himself, before he'd lost his way in the woods.

Thomas said, "That introduces us all, then, so no need for this any longer."

He snuffed the candle, and the room descended again into darkness.

Chapter 2

Alec awoke to the creak of the door at the top of the mine shaft, the sound of it opening now familiar after several days spent in the dank, close underground chamber. He rolled over on his narrow bunk with a groan, even the glimmer of light visible on the floor making him squint.

A voice called down, echoing slightly. "Up and at 'em, boys! We've made the arrangements, and those of you such as are able will be learning today how to make nails to earn your living. Ladder's down; you're needed up."

This was followed by a horrid clanging that had everyone below groaning and coming to their feet, moving toward the only evidence of a world of sunlight and open skies.

Thomas reached the bottom of the shaft and shouted up irritably, "All right already, Jonas! Put away the pots and stop with the din."

The clanging stopped, and he turned back to look at the men crowding around behind him, taking a count by eye. His eyes narrowed into a pinched expression.

"Where's William?"

Benjamin shook his head in disgust, his scraggly, gray beard flying, and called over his shoulder as he turned back into the gloom. "I'll go and roust him, the lazy sod."

He was back in a moment, and Alec knew instantly that

the grim expression on the older man's face could portend nothing good. "William ain't coming. He's gone and escaped from here, into the hereafter, the lucky blighter."

Alec saw Robert grin merrily and poke the man next to him in the ribs. "See? I wasn't the next, after all."

Thomas ignored Robert, digesting Benjamin's statement, and gave a disgusted frown. He called up to the surface, "You've lost another one, Jonas. Best send down the litter, and stand ready to heave him back up. I'll help you dig a grave for him before we start in with making nails."

Alec heard a muffled curse from the guard, and Thomas turned back, gathering him and Benjamin up with a jerk of his chin. "Come with me, and help me bring him over here."

Alec swallowed hard, but went along without a word.

Benjamin noted the younger man's discomfort and clapped him on the shoulder. "Seems a waste of effort, I know, to haul a man back aboveground, only to put him back into the earth up there, but trust me, this way smells better."

Alec shuddered, but said nothing and followed the other two men to the corner where William had been sleeping.

Despite the darkness away from the shaft, Alec could see William's huddled corpse curled up under a thin blanket, barred to the last from the use of a bunk. Alec wondered to himself whether the chill of the floor had hastened the man's end.

Benjamin lifted the blanket off of the dead man and looked him over, folding the covering absently and setting it on the nearest table. "I think his shoes will fit you, Alec, and they look to be in better condition than the ones you have." He turned to Thomas. "Least old William can do for Alec in exchange for the service of heaving him up is to give over the shoes he's no use for any longer, eh?"

Thomas nodded his approval. "Go ahead and swap them out, if you like. He'll bury just as well with worn-out shoes as with new." He glanced back to where the other men stood, milling about under the light from above. "Do it quick-like, though, and let's get him moved."

Alec looked at the shoes on the dead man's feet and swallowed hard again.

Although they were definitely in better condition than the scraps of leather that clung to his own feet, he didn't want to admit to these men that he had a deep-seated fear of being around death.

After letting a shudder roll down his spine, though, he gritted his teeth and bent to the task, slipping the shoes from the lifeless feet. The dead man's skin was cold to the touch, almost waxy, and his ankles moved stiffly as Alec pulled each shoe off. He was glad that he'd not yet broken his fast, because he could feel his stomach protesting at the sensation.

As he pulled William's second shoe off, he saw something glinting faintly in the heel. He reached in curiously and felt what could only be a coin, though he could not discern what its denomination might be in the darkness. Doing his best to not reveal the discovery, he tilted the shoe down as he put it on the floor, letting the coin slide back down toward its toe.

He kicked off his own worn-out footwear and stepped into the dead man's shoes. The fit was acceptable, though he thought he could feel a lingering chill from the cold flesh that had last worn them.

"Hurry it up, boy!" Thomas' hiss was impatient, but

Benjamin put a steadying hand on Alec's shoulder.

"You've come out ahead in this, friend, and William wouldn't begrudge you. He'd have done the same, had it been the other way around." The old man chuckled. "I only wish that William had still had the fine regimental coat he used to boast of. It would have kept the chill off my old bones quite nicely."

Alec shuddered again, and pushed his old shoes onto the unresisting feet without further ceremony. Thomas bent and put his hands under one of the dead man's arms, while Benjamin positioned himself on the other side.

"You get his feet, Alec. Ready now? Hup!"

The three men stood with their load and shuffled over the floor awkwardly, their load at once oddly loose in its movements, and stiff under their fingers. Alec knew that it would be a long time before he could dispel the memory of the dead man's head lolling back between his shoulders.

By the time they got back under the opening to the outside with William's remains, a crudely-built litter was bumping its way down the shaft, stout ropes secured at its corners. The trio wordlessly loaded their burden onto it, and secured William's corpse with the loose ends of hempen line that lay beside the litter where it had settled onto the floor.

Jonas called down, his voice betraying a hint of worry. "Make sure that you tie him on there good. I'll not have him falling from halfway up and doing dishonor to his remains."

"Aye," Thomas called back up to the guard. "We've got him well secured. You may bring him up when you are ready."

Alec could hear Jonas calling out overhead.

"Timothy! Lawrence! Come and help me with this."

After a moment, the rope tightened as the three men overhead finished the job that the men underground had begun, hauling William up into the light. The last thing that Alec saw of the dead man was his big toe, sticking out through the battered shoe that Alec had pushed onto his foot. It was blue-white in the light shining down from aboveground, and again, Alec was glad for his empty stomach.

Chapter 3

Making nails was easier than digging graves, Alec thought. On the other hand, there was a limit to how many graves he might be called upon to dig, while there seemed no end to the work of hammering out and cutting the iron stock for nails.

He'd had to help dig two graves now – Robert had outlived William by less than a fortnight – but he'd lost count of the nails he had shaped after the first day on the forge and anvil. He guessed that it numbered in the dozens, and he had only gotten faster at it in the weeks that had followed.

It developed that Benjamin had been employed as a nail maker before the war, and had been able to teach all of those who wanted to trade the chill, dark boredom of life underground for sweaty, hard labor with a hammer and tongs in hand.

As an added inducement, those who worked were relieved of their manacles. At first, it had only been while they were aboveground, but over the weeks, the guards had relaxed enough to leave them off the prisoners entirely.

Some had refused to work—the British soldier Miller among them—and the guard had shrugged, muttering something about letting the prisoners work things out amongst themselves. Miller had been called up by name the next morning, though, and none had seen him since. There were whispers that he'd been executed, although Alec thought that the prisoners would have been required to dig yet another grave, had that been the case.

Whatever had happened to Miller, it had driven the few defaulters to step up and do their part, even if they weren't particularly well-suited to the labor. There was no small amount of grumbling when they'd finally learned that Miller had been paroled, and might even then be on his way home. Most of the prisoners seemed to think that the incident had been manufactured to encourage universal participation in their labors.

For his part, though, Alec had gladly joined in from the start, and soon grew to actually enjoy the routine of heating the strip of bar iron, pounding it to a taper at one end, and then folding and cutting it with well-placed blows from his hammer.

He'd drop the pointed end into a hole in the anvil, and then give a few more strokes of the hammer to shape the head, and then move the finished nail into the water to cool before fishing it out and tossing it into an open barrel, where it rang off the others already inside.

Benjamin spoke wistfully of machines he'd heard of that took the place of a dozen men or more, replacing the labor of hammering by means of massive blades that cut a long plate of steel into tapered shapes, then needing only to have their heads hammered out. Of course, such a device was far too expensive to justify, when the labor of prisoners could take its place.

Not to mention, of course, that it was considered risky enough to put hammers and hot iron into the hands of prisoners who had already proven once that accidents could befall a man among their number who could not be trusted. A machine that could cut straight through a steel plate could doubtless be employed to arrange for even more gruesome mishaps than could a pair of scissors.

A bead of sweat made its way down Alec's forehead as the combined heat of the forge and the summer sun started to become too much for him. He raised his hand up to call for relief, and Clem hurried over to sprinkle tallow over the nails he'd made in this shift.

The scrawny lad used a stout stick to stir the nails and distribute the melted grease over them. It would preserve the metal against rust, and adding it had been about the only job that Clem was suited to perform. Another prisoner, a burly man who had introduced himself only as Gus, came and took the heavy hammer out of Alec's hand.

For his part, Alec gratefully walked into the shade provided by a small shack, and dipped himself a cool, clean drink of water out of a bucket there. He didn't mind that it spilled down his front – it provided additional respite from the heat.

Of course, Alec knew that he ought savor the heat while it afflicted him, as he would shortly go back down belowground, where the temperature was nearly unchanged all the year around. Until the guards spotted that he had stopped working at the forge, he took his ease in the light of a spring day, enjoying the simple sight of puffy clouds in a crystalline blue sky.

He glanced up at the guardhouse at the corner of the high fence that surrounded the opening to the mine, and saw Jonas looking back at him alertly. Though the guards had been somewhat more humane with their charges since the income from their nail-making had started to flow in, they had been no less wary of a jailbreak.

Alec saw Jonas motion to another guard – Alec thought his name was Gad – and prepared himself to be ushered back under the earth. Whenever the men were not actively laboring, they were kept within the walls of rock and dirt, under a roof of dozens of feet of the same.

Given the stories that Thomas had passed along late at night, though, Alec could understand their concern. In addition to the attempt when the prisoners had used mining as a cover for digging an escape tunnel out of the compound, there was a long history of escapes or attempted escapes from the mine. The very first prisoner housed here was said to have simply climbed up a rope dropped down a second shaft that was unguarded.

Alec wondered idly whether Thomas was passing the stories around to get a sense of who might be interested in pursuing another escape, but in truth, he couldn't imagine that breaking out of the prison would be possible, as it stood now.

Entry and exit to the mine were through an iron-barred door that stood within the guardhouse, and no fewer than two guards stood watch over it, even at night. When he passed near to the shaft end of the underground crypt, Alec could hear them talking with each other at all hours and playing word games to pass the time and keep themselves alert.

Gad approached and called out, "Prisoner, show your hands."

Alec raised his hands to show that they were empty, but replied crossly, "I have a name that you can use to address me, like a human being, and not the animal that you take me for." The pleasant feeling of seeing sun and sky had evaporated in a moment at the guard's tone and words.

"Aye, but I need not concern myself overmuch with learning it, prisoner. You are a traitor to your country, and as such, the way I figure it, you've declared to the world that you've no more humanity than a common roadside cur."

Gad made a show of looking Alec over, taking in his ragged clothing and utter lack of hygiene. Alec felt suddenly self-conscious of the spare beard that had started to gather about his cheeks and chin, and wished for the hundredth time that they would be permitted the occasional services of a barber.

The guard nodded slowly and thoughtfully. "In any event, prisoner," he took care to emphasize the word, "I rather doubt that you'll last long enough to bother coming to know your name. You have a lean and sickly look about you, and I shouldn't be surprised if you're the next to be planted yonder." He jerked his chin toward the makeshift graveyard where William and Robert lay, and Alec felt an angry chill of shock settle over him.

"Were I in your position, I should be rather more concerned with my own well-being, guard." Alec glanced about at the other prisoners visible aboveground meaningfully. "You lot may be armed, but there are more of us than of you, if it comes to it." He spat at the man's feet, heedless of the danger of provoking a man who held a musket, while he stood in rags. The guard's words had hit a nerve.

Gad scowled and brought his arm about, delivering a clout to Alec's head, staggering him. "Shut your yap, prisoner, and stop stalling your return to the ground where you belong."

Alec sullenly complied, but marked the other man's face in his mind. As he let himself be led into the guardhouse, through the kitchen, and directed down the ladder to the dank and dark prison room, he fixed a determination to live longer than his new antagonist, no matter what he had to do to ensure it.

Chapter 4

The clanging of pots woke Alec with a jolt, and he heard the other men around him stirring and groaning as well. Today, it was Benjamin who stumbled over to the entrance shaft and shouted up, irritably, "We're awake, ye demons!"

Alec recognized the answering voice as Jonas'. "Send Alexander Tinsmith — er, Tinsworth — up to the surface at once. He is needed for an urgent matter."

Alec cursed and swung to his feet. Naught but ill could possibly come of such a summons.

"Alec is on his way," Benjamin called up, and motioned Alec toward the ladder with his hand. As Alec passed, Benjamin put his hand on the younger man's shoulder and spoke quietly. "Worry not, lad. It's likely some small matter that they want to talk over with you. You've nothing to hide, nor anything that any of that lot can make you feel shame over. I'll see you on your return."

Alec had never thought it possible that going up the ladder into the light of day could make him feel a sense of impending doom, rather than the normal feeling of jubilance at being relieved of the dark and the smell of the chamber behind him. By the time he reached the top of the ladder, though, his heart was pounding in his throat, and it was all he could do to keep a quaver out of his voice as he spoke through the iron grate in the door at the top of the ladder.

"Alec Tinsworth, as commanded."

Jonas swung a lantern around to peer into the darkness behind Alec and ensure that he was alone at the top of the ladder, then unbolted and swung open the door.

Alec emerged into the kitchen, his eyes squinted nearly shut as usual at the brightness of the morning light streaming in through the windows. After the door banged shut behind him, causing him to jump at how loud it was at this proximity, Jonas spoke.

"You've a visitor," he said, and indicated with a gesture of his hand that Alec should precede him out of the kitchen and into the guardhouse.

As he passed through the guards' quarters, Alec was struck at how similarly their space was laid out to the underground quarters of the prisoners. Tables and benches lined one wall, and bunks were arrayed along the other. And yet, the feeling of the space in which they walked felt completely different, due only to the presence of light and fresh air.

Of course, the door through which they emerged into the full sunshine of the morning also was different. No iron grate stood upon it, nor any heavy bolt controlled from without. These reflections, though, occupied just one corner of Alec's mind, as he wondered who might have learned that he was in this prison, and who would be bothered to visit him here.

At the gate to the wall about the prison space, he got his answer in a rush of recognition at the tall, spare form of his father, who was speaking with another of the guards there. A traveling cloak hung loosely around him, and Alec was shocked to see that his hair had gone from the jet black he remembered to an aged-looking white in the span of just a year since he'd last seen the man.

When his father turned to face him, Alec was reassured, however, to see that the same firmness of purpose and lively attentiveness to every detail around him still animated his father's face.

Heedless of Jonas' instructions now, Alec rushed forward and embraced his father tightly. The tears that stained his face might have been shameful on another day, but he permitted himself to feel nothing but joy at this reunion.

After a startled moment, his father returned Alec's embrace, and Alec could practically feel the man counting his ribs as his hand passed up and down his son's back. He felt no judgment from his father's touch, though – only a building fury, thankfully directed at someone else.

However, he could hear his father's restraint as he said simply, emotion held carefully in check, "'Tis good to see you, son, and to know that you are hale and hearty."

Alec stepped back and returned the oddly formal greeting. "It is good to see you, as well, Father. This is no heaven on Earth, but it is better than a swift and unlooked-for passage to the hereafter."

The elder Tinsworth nodded at Alec's words, and then turned to the guard. "May we have a moment's privacy? I've news to relate to my son, of a strictly personal nature, with no possible military application."

The guard pursed his lips, but nodded and withdrew to a distance just out of earshot.

Alec's father closed his eyes in evident pain as he spoke. "I am sorry to tell you that my errand here is not solely to learn of your health, son. As soon as I learned that you were held captive in this place, I came here to inform you that your mother was taken ill as the first snow flew, and she was gone before the new year began. You and I are all that remain of the Tinsworth family."

Alec was aware of the breath passing into his chest and back out through his nose, and of the blood roaring in his ears. He could feel the solid weight of the earth pressing back against his shoes, the passing breeze stirring his hair and bringing a chill over his skin. The breeze brought a faint smell of freshly-turned soil from somewhere, and the lingering smell of charcoal from the forges.

He was aware of the tears streaming down his face, by the chill they left behind in the breeze, and he heard someone asking in his own voice, "I pray that she did not suffer?"

His father looked grave but shook his head. "Her greatest suffering was in not knowing whether you had joined your brothers in your own grave. I feel certain that she is at peace now, knowing that you are still alive and in relative safety away from the hazards of wartime violence."

The part of Alec's mind that was still working made a conscious decision to not remind his father that both his brothers had died, not of violence visited upon them by their rebellious neighbors, but of the illnesses that ran through encampments like wildfire through a drought-stricken wood. The hazard remained a very real one in his current condition of captivity, but it would serve no purpose whatsoever to bring his father's mind back to this bitter fact.

He felt himself nod, again as though it were someone else moving him like a puppet on strings. "With the house and Mother gone, where are you staying now?"

"I have taken lodging with a friend near to here, whose

name I will not utter where it might cause her to come to grief for having proven a true supporter of those of us who have chosen the honorable and righteous path of loyalty to our sovereign. There are some few of us who share refuge under her roof, along with her daughters, and together we rejoice in what victories there are to celebrate."

Alec was starting to feel that he might be regaining mastery of himself now, though his eyes burned and his nose streamed uncontrolled with his continued tears. "I am relieved to hear, Father, that you have found a place of safety in this unsettled and disturbed land. What of your business?"

His father shook his head curtly. "Gone. All was seized up by the so-called 'Committee of Safety,' though whose safety they are supposed to be ensuring, I cannot perceive. It seems more likely that they are looking to the safety of their own pocketbooks, as they seem to have all done quite well for themselves in the disposition of our expropriated properties and personal goods."

An old anger threatened to overtake the older man, and Alec could see him master it in an effort of will, and he made a dismissive gesture with his hand. "'Tis all but things, though, and things can be replaced with a sufficient desire and application." He took his son's shoulder in his hand. "My true legacy, however, stands before me, and that is a greater blessing than I could have hoped for today."

He looked Alec over again, and grimaced slightly. "I can see that they are scarcely feeding you here, and your personal needs have been neglected completely. My landlady's elder daughter is a fair hand with a razor, and I'm of a mind to send her around to see to you."

He motioned to the guard, bidding him to come close again. "Would you fellows have any objection to my sending a girl around to see to the barber's duties for my boy?"

The guard considered for a moment, and then answered, "I don't see why not, so long as she don't mind being watched closely to ensure that she is not supplying him with a secreted blade or other weapons. Indeed, if any of the others here should wish to avail themselves, we have a small provision for such, if she be willing to supply their needs under the same conditions."

Alec's father nodded sharply. "I have no doubt that she would be all too happy to do so."

Jonas' eyes narrowed thoughtfully, and he added, "She ought be aware, though, that we house not only traitors to the American nation, but some few hard criminals, and we cannot vouchsafe her security within our walls."

Tinsworth nodded gravely. "I shall be sure to tell her that, as well. She is a well-informed young woman, and I have little doubt that she is sensible of the dangers attendant to visiting a place so infamous as your prison here has become."

The guard bristled visibly at Alec's father's words, but said only, "'Tis only prudent that she should know."

Alec gave this exchange only the slightest attention, as it was not nearly as important as the news that his father had come and found him in this forsaken place for the purpose of delivering. He'd known that his mother was frail, and that the shocks of the past years of rebellion had been difficult for her to bear. When his brothers had together joined the king's men and gone off to defend the supremacy of the Crown and Parliament over their restive colonies, she had taken to her bed for a week.

Then word came back that both brothers had succumbed to an unidentified camp fever within hours of one another, and offering no comfort beyond the cold statement that they had not suffered long, nor been felled by a ball or blade aimed by one of their erstwhile neighbors. She had remained in her room for a solid month, and had only started to come down for dinner every few days when the committee's representatives had arrived at their door and demanded that they vacate the premises at once.

Alec had decided shortly thereafter to take his brothers' place in the loyal militia, and he could not escape now the horrid thought that his departure – and his subsequent disappearance – had been the final stroke that had finished the job of sapping his mother's will to live.

Having come to this terrible conclusion, he heard his father saying to him, "Alec, I must take my leave now, as they told me that I could only speak with you until the beginning of your duties for the day. As I see your fellows emerging from underground, I surmise that you are needed at your assigned tasks, and that the time allotted for our interview has ended. I shall send the girl around to see to you, and shall try to visit you myself from time to time. It is the least that I can do for you, until this wretched affair is brought to a happy conclusion, and we are restored of our property and position."

He extended his hand to Alec, who stared at it dumbly for a time, until he realized that his father meant for him to shake it, in lieu of the overly-familiar embrace with which he had been greeted.

He took the proffered hand and clasped it for a moment. "Thank you, Father, for coming to find me here, and for sharing with me the unhappy news of home. I shall hope to see you again soon under happier circumstances."

His father gave his hand a last squeeze, and then Alec watched him turn around and leave, free to leave this place of bondage, if not an entirely free man.

After the gate closed behind Alec's father, Jonas turned to him, a look of sympathetic understanding on his face. "Couldn't help but overhear. Lost your mother. We can spare you from your duties today, if you need."

Alec did not reply, but the tears started down his face again, giving far more certain confirmation than any words might have done.

Jonas nodded. "Lost mine at the beginning of the war, after the blockade stopped up our trade, and we had trouble finding enough to eat for a bit. Then the pox came through, and I lost my sister, too, and my brother lost his wife, who was with child at the time. This war's hard on us all."

Alec didn't know why, but he felt moved to confess the enormity of his crime against his mother to the guard. His eyes streaming, he said bitterly, "Aye, 'tis, but you didn't bring about any of those deaths. I alone am to blame for my mother's demise, and I alone will answer for it when I stand before my maker."

He turned without another word and walked back to the guardhouse, where he waited silently for Jonas to let him back down through the iron door, into the comforting darkness below. As he descended into the earth, he felt as though he were passing by the spirits of his brothers, judged and found wanting by them both.

Further down, he could almost hear his mother speaking to him. "Stand tall, Alec," she'd said to him so often that he could hear the proud catch in her voice even now.

How could he ever stand tall again, proud of his name, proud of his family, proud of their faithfulness to their king, proud of his service and that of his brothers, knowing that he'd brought all of it to ruin, that he would never again hear her urge him on?

He went to his bunk and pulled the thin blanket there over himself, wishing that he could go back to sleep and never need wake to his guilt again.

Chapter 5

Waking in the familiar gloom, the smell of smoldering charcoal oppressive, Alec felt as though he'd not slept at all. Around him, he could hear the other prisoners moving about, eating a meal – breakfast or supper, he could not tell at first – and talking quietly amongst themselves.

From the few words he overheard, he decided that they were finished with their day of work, and he'd slept the day through. However, he did not stir from his bunk just yet, wanting to stay a while longer with the dreams that had kept him company while he'd slept.

He could not remember them clearly, but he felt that his mother had come and visited him in them, offering some reassurance that she, at least, did not place any blame on him for her death. He grimaced to himself. He could not forgive himself so easily, but she had always been quicker to find the way of mercy for him than he had been for himself.

He remembered an instance when he and his brothers had been engaging in horseplay in the house, despite both their parents' repeated commands to save such for out of doors, when disaster had struck. He'd tried to dodge a surprise grab from Michael from behind the doorway to the dining room, and he'd misjudged his step.

The cabinet full of his mother's best dinner service – most of it brought over from London at his father's behest and very great expense – had arrested his fall, but there was nothing to stop the fall of an even dozen pieces of the precious Stafford shire earthenware until it reached the floor and shattered. Michael had taken one look and had fled outdoors, leaving Alec to his fate.

Alec could remember with perfect clarity the seemingly endless array of jagged pieces of blue-and-white ceramic, jumbled hopelessly together across the wide boards of the dining room floor. He'd not even attempted to flee the punishment he knew would follow as he heard his mother's footsteps approach, followed by the heavier tread of his father's footfalls.

She'd rounded the corner, and given a small gasp at the sight, her hand flying to her mouth. Her other hand, though, she had immediately flung up behind her, restraining her husband and preventing him for a moment from even seeing the scene of destruction.

Alec had averted his eyes, looking down at the floor, his gaze caught by a larger fragment decorated with what looked like nothing so much as an accusing eye staring back up at him from the floor. When he dared to glance up again, he saw that his father had now come into view, his mother's fingers curled over his shoulder, her own eyes bright with unshed tears.

His father seemed to have grown larger and more menacing in the moment since he'd come around the corner into the dining room, and his face was a blotchy red. Alec looked past his face, though, to the delicate fingers on his shoulder, restraining all his rage with no more than a few ounces' worth of pressure.

Some unspoken communication passed between his parents in that moment, and Alec could see his father's rage dissipate and his form seemed almost to deflate before his eyes. With nearly perfect restraint, he'd said softly and dangerously, "Alexander, go up to your bed, and don't let me lay eyes on you for the rest of the day."

Alec had looked to his mother, and she'd nodded swift agreement, almost as though she were a co-conspirator enabling him to escape greater punishment for his misdeed. He could tell, though, that the hand clenched before her mouth was to stop herself from crying out at the loss of her treasured possessions to a moment's inattention.

All through that long, solitary day, Alec had let the guilt at what he'd cost his mother wash over him. When hunger twisted in his belly, he'd welcomed it as the deserved consequence for carelessly failing to mind the oft-repeated admonitions about racing about the house with his brothers.

Long after dusk had settled down, as the first light of a waning moon shone in through the window, the door had quietly opened, and his mother had entered, a plate in her hand. She had regained her composure since the morning, and sat wordlessly beside him on his bed.

After a long, thoughtful silence, she spoke, very gently. "I know, Alec, that you did not mean to knock down the serving dishes. I know, too, that were it within your power to restore them, to somehow reverse your actions, you would do so." She sighed deeply. "However, no man can unbreak what is broken, and no clock has yet been built that runs backward for our convenience."

She placed the plate on Alec's lap, and he could see that it bore bread and cheese, and a thick slice of cold meat. He pushed aside the eager grumble of his belly, though, to give full attention to his mother's continued soft words.

"I'll not deny that I am sorely saddened to see so much of your father's efforts to secure my joy dashed to pieces in a thoughtless moment. He knows that I take pride at being able to set a genteel table when we have company, and after the very first time that I exclaimed over the fine platters at another house's table, he ordered from the finest merchant in London some of the items that were lost today."

She looked away for a moment, gazing at the moon, and in its light, Alec could again see tears straining to overflow the bottom of her brightly-reflected eyes. She turned back to him, though, and continued. "Now, the deed will have to suffice for the thing, as there is no replacing such items at any price any more, with the current disruptions to the trade."

She shrugged. "And so, my son, you must learn a difficult lesson at the cost of my pain. The effects of some acts cannot be made better, and the only way to avoid paying the cost of them is to refrain from engaging in the acts in the first place."

It was then Alec's tears that trickled down his cheeks, and he finally spoke. "I am so sorry, mother. I am just so . . . sorry."

She nodded and reached out to stroke his cheek, her thumb brushing away a tear there. "I know you are, Alec, and I'll have to let you just be sorry, as there is aught you can do to make your error right. I will tell you something, though, that you probably do not know."

He looked up at her sharply, his expression curious. "Oh?"

"This is not the first time that one of the good platters has been broken. Not long after the first of the ones your father had made was delivered, I was putting it away after washing it, and it slipped out of my fingers and fell to the table. It was no more than a hand span, but 'twas enough to split the platter right in two."

Alec's mouth dropped open and she nodded. "I was beside myself, thinking that your father would be furious at the waste. But I'll tell you now what he told me then, and let it be a balm for your worries. He told me that they were but things, and that things could be replaced with a sufficient desire and application."

Recalling now, as he lay in his bunk, that his father had said almost the same thing to him when he'd visited that morning, Alec bit his lip to stop himself from weeping yet again.

He remembered that his mother had left him that night with an embrace and the plate of food to eat alone in the moonlight, and he realized that though she had been the bearer of mercy, it had been his father's wisdom that had delivered him of the worst of his self-recriminations.

Thinking about the bread and cheese his mother had brought to him so many years ago, though, reminded him that he hadn't eaten at all today, and so he reluctantly rose from the bunk.

Thomas nodded in somber greeting as Alec came to the table. "Heard what happened, friend. Saved your ration for you." Thomas pushed a tin plate with a bit of cold porridge and a hard crust of bread across the table to him, and Alec felt a rush of warmth toward the man, knowing how tempting an extra mouthful of food was after a long day at work.

Another prisoner – for the life of him, Alec couldn't remember his name – moved aside on the bench to make room for Alec to sit. Doing his best to keep his emotions out of his voice, Alec said simply, "Thank you for understanding."

Thomas nodded. "Of course, boy. Time'll come when you have some opportunity to show one of us a kindness, and I've no doubt you'll do so with all your heart. You're a good lad, and you've been done hard by."

He glanced around at the other prisoners around the table. "Of course, we've near all been done hard by, one way or another, I suppose." He spoke more quietly, almost as though he feared that the guard at the top of the mine shaft might hear him, and added, "Time'll come, too, when we may have an opportunity to even the scales a bit, but that's a conversation for another time."

He motioned to the plate in front of Alec. "Eat your food, and try to get some rest tonight. Although you may have slept the day, I don't doubt that your spirit is weary, and you'll sleep the night through. Tomorrow, as they say, is a new day – and whether 'tis to be a day of torment or a day for a new opportunity is anyone's guess. But to find out, we must reach it first, and deal with whatever it may bring to us, eh?"

He stood and came around the table, clapping Alec on the shoulder as he passed. "I'm for bed, and the depths of philosophy can wait until morning."

Chapter 6

Despite Thomas' reassurances, Alec did not sleep well that night, tossing and turning, waking every time one of the men stirred in the night. By the next morning, he was bleary-eyed as they sat together to break their fast around the long, coarse table.

It was just as well that the light was nearly nonexistent down here, as the food sent down from one meal to the next might be anywhere from merely unappetizing to actively disgusting. This morning's offering was merely cheap – some loaves of stale Indian-corn bread, and a soup that relied mostly on boiled cabbage, but which might have seen some scrawny bits of chicken at some point. It washed down well enough, though, with shared bottles of cider, though even that had gone off a bit, and some of the bottles tasted as though they were partway to vinegar.

In any event, it was enough to rouse weary men and give them the strength to climb the ladder under Gad's baleful eye.

Those assigned aboveground for the morning took up their stations and began the day's work, stoking the forges and working the bellows to bring them up to working temperature. Alec was working on moving iron stock over by the forge for easier access when he tripped, his feet still feeling heavy and uncoordinated.

The iron clattered into the churned-up mud at Benjamin's feet, where he stood working a bellows, and the older man shouted at him. "Have a care, boyo, lest you smash my foot into splinters. Those aren't saplings you're tossing about."

Alec's head was ducked down in shame, and he was starting to apologize when Thomas called out, "Go easy on the lad, Benjamin. You know how his night went."

"Aye, I know that he was excused from work yesterday, which left the rest of us to make up for his absence, and I know that he nearly ruined me just now. We've all suffered in this war, and our confinement and labor here is but one part of that suffering."

His tone softened, though, and he turned to Alec. "I know you're hurting, boy, but do try not to manifest your pain in injury to the rest of us."

Alec nodded, stacking the iron stock back in his arms. It was heavy and awkward, but he managed to deliver it to the work bench next to the forge without further incident.

Thomas approached him. "Are you up to swinging a hammer today, or would it be better for you to work the bellows?"

Alec considered his fellow prisoner. "I believe that I can trust myself to work before the forge, rather than behind it," he said finally.

Thomas nodded, but didn't say anything further, moving into his position and nodding curtly for Alec to begin the process of creating nails out of iron bar stock.

The relative mindlessness of the task left Alec able to think from time to time about the events of the prior day. With his mother and brothers gone, and their property all but dispossessed of them, what would hold Alec and his father here on these shores? Presuming, of course, that Alec could survive his captivity to the end of the war, and that its conclusion would permit them any mobility to make a choice, might it be best for them to plan to return to the mother country?

His hammer rang clean and true, stroke after weary stroke, and it wasn't long before he was wishing he could catch Gad's eye and let himself be led back to the iron portal that led underground, where he could let his shaking arms recover for a while.

A few days past, though, the guards had decided that it made more sense to switch out the whole team working each anvil at once, and so they regularized the shifts that the prisoners worked. This was more fair, Alec had to admit, but it did mean that he often now had to drive himself past his natural point of endurance before he could get relief.

Eventually, though, Gad cracked the horsewhip he liked to use to signal the prisoners – and which he seemed to wish he could use directly on them – and Alec gratefully put the finishing blows on the nail he was working, and dropped it into its waiting barrel. He put the hammer and tongs down, wiped the sweat from his brow, and went to the well for a dipper full of ice-cold water.

Jonas emerged from the guardhouse and motioned Alec over. When the prisoner stopped before him, he said conversationally, "Your father sent word over that he would be dispatching his friend's daughter here in three days' time to act barber to you, and to any of the other men such as should like to engage her services for a modest fee."

Alec nodded, frowning slightly to himself at the fact that his father had corresponded with the guard, and not his own son.

The guard continued, though, heedless of Alec's reaction. "She's relatively new to the trade, and but a girl, so I should think that a fee of one shilling for those who need their beards cut and shaved is more than fair, while those who wish only to have their hair trimmed up in neat fashion can do so for sixpence. He assures me that she is quite capable of working the day long, if there be sufficient demand."

Alec frowned more visibly now. "How are we to pay her?" He was aware of the cool pressure of William's secreted coin against the toes of his left foot, still embedded into the leather of the shoe he'd gotten as an impromptu inheritance. However, to his knowledge, he was the only one of the prisoners who held any sort of cash.

Jonas made a dismissive gesture with his hand, however. "It can be paid out of the earnings from your nail-making, if you've no other funds available to you, and if your families should prove unwilling or unable to provide for you in the this regard."

Alec hadn't been aware that they had earnings from the nail-making work. He'd just assumed that the prisoners were acting as slave laborers, with no more benefit to themselves than the foul food they were haphazardly provided.

He kept his thoughts to himself, though, and Jonas concluded, "I trust that you will let it be known among the men that they are permitted and encouraged to avail themselves of the young woman's services as barber. You've become a wild-looking lot, and I won't deny that it would be a relief to look you over and not see hairy beasts staring back at me."

He pointed toward the door of the guardhouse. "You may return to your bunk and tell your fellows what I've asked you to pass along."

Alec nodded and turned to leave.

"Oh, there is one other thing," Jonas called. "Your father

asked that I pass along to you that Miss Landry is most eager to resume her acquaintance with you as she works."

Alec took pride in his ability to refrain from reacting outwardly, but he could still feel his ears burning as he walked away and made his way past the watchful eye of the guard at the iron door and down the ladder to rest in the darkness.

Miss Landry! His father was up to his old tricks again.

Miss Holly Landry was, perhaps, a year his junior, and while she had been no great beauty when Alec had gone off to join the militia, she was also not unpleasant to pass time with.

His father had found ways to arrange for the two of them to spend a surprising amount of time together, and while they got along well enough, that had been the extent of it. She was rather more forceful in her opinions – and in her manner of expressing them – than he was accustomed to or comfortable with.

The last time he'd seen Miss Landry had been just a few weeks prior to the arrival of word of his brothers' deaths. She had been holding forth on the best way to force the capitulation of the American forces.

"It is quite simple, I should think. We've a large enough force of men under arms to encircle them and drive them against some substantial body of water – I rather think that the Atlantic ocean in January should suffice – and give them the choice of jumping in as free men, or laying down their arms and returning to the sweet embrace of loyalty to their sovereign."

Alec hadn't risen to the argument, lacking the knowledge to counter her assumptions, but now he knew all too well how impractical it would be to attempt to encircle the American forces as she had envisioned. They would slip like ghosts through any line that did not consist of men standing at fingertip-length from one another – and might even find a way to outfox a picket that close.

What he had said, though, was simply, "I suspect that, given that choice, all too many of them would choose to jump in and drown free – and that their partisans all the country round would then denounce us as murderers and worse. Furthermore, this is no longer a simple contest between our King and a rabble here, but a true war between ourselves and our old enemies, being decided on our shores."

Miss Landry had huffed angrily. "What did the French think they were doing, interfering in a local insurrection? Have we ever so openly involved ourselves in their internal affairs? It is beyond all tolerance."

He answered dryly, "I am sure that they were only too happy to have the opportunity to disrupt the internal felicity of the British Kingdom for their own amusement, quite aside from the opportunity to strike back at us for their defeat in the late war here with their savage allies."

Miss Landry shuddered delicately. "I have heard the tales of that war from my Papa, and I am quite glad that our agents among the Indians seem to have secured their alliance with us in the present conflict. Why, I should not feel safe in my bed at night, were I to fear the sorts of attacks he told me they favored."

"Aye, many of their nations have sided with us, but not all, so don't sleep too soundly, Miss Landry," Alec's father said, a mischievous twinkle in his eye.

Alec shook his head at Miss Landry's theatrical gasp, and put a hand on her arm, and he did not miss the deepening twinkle in his father's eyes. "There is no need for worry, Miss Landry. Those Indian nations who have chosen the wrong side of this contest are far removed from this place, and in any event, none have dared to raid this close to the cities in a decade and longer."

Miss Landry turned to him. "I do trust that you know of what you speak, Mister Tinsworth."

"I have it on the authority of my brothers that we shall come to no harm at the hands of the Indians in these parts, under any foreseeable circumstances."

The smile that had creased the corners of his father's eyes in that moment was, he realized now, the last time he'd seen the man smile at anything. With the reverse of the family's fortunes, he wondered whether he should ever see his father smile at anything again.

Chapter 7

When the morning of Miss Landry's barber service came around, it felt to Alec like some sort of holiday. He and the handful of others who had "paid" by making their mark in Jonas' account-book were excused from their nail-making duties until the afternoon, and were queued up eagerly, awaiting her arrival.

Most had opted to spend the shilling and six to get both haircut and shave, and as Alec looked around the group, he thought that some were getting their money's worth more than others. Most of the prisoners had declined to join them, either because they were sending what little they could earn to family dependent on their income, or, in a few loud-mouthed cases, because they refused to have a woman serve as their barber.

Even among the men who had agreed to have Miss Landry attend to them, there was some suspicion about her suitability to the task. One old thief among them, a wiry man named Richard, chuckled to the men gathered to await her arrival, "I shouldn't wonder but that she be a powerfully unattractive woman, the kind who'd've been burnt a witch back in the old days."

Alec had frowned, saying, "She was a plain young woman, when I knew her, at least, but not hideous to behold."

"Is she the type what is drawn to dandy men, then, out of spite to her father?"

"Nay, she is a proper and respectable gentlewoman, from a good family, and enjoyed happy relations with her parents." He glared around at the men. "'Tis shameful to hear you lot speculate on her base reasons for coming to our aid in this place. When no proper barber will come to our service, desiring instead to leave us in a state of barbaric nature, we ought be only grateful to any who would brave the gates of our prison, that we may face what proscribed part of the world we can see as men, rather than as beasts."

He realized that his voice had risen when he saw Gad look up sharply and stroll over to the group.

"Problem, fellows?" The guard looked around at each of the abruptly stony faces with malevolent suspicion. "We can always turn your barber away at the gate, and put you boys back to your proper work, if her presence here threatens our domestic peace."

None of the prisoners responded to his goading, and eventually, he sniffed and strode off to stand with the other guard, resuming their quiet conversation. The guffaws of the two guards seemed to be at the prisoners' expense, given the crude gestures and sidewise glances they shot at the men, but all were long used to ignoring this variety of abuse.

From the gate at the fence, the prisoners could hear the guard call out a challenge to someone approaching, and they fell into the very picture of rectitude and good order.

The gate swung open, and a pair of figures entered.

The first, Alec recognized at once as Miss Landry's papa, though like his own father, the man was shockingly aged in the scant year since they'd sat around the table, speculating on the progress of the war and the threat of Indian allies to the American and French forces. Where he'd once been stout, nearly rotund, he was now much reduced, and the skin of his jowls hung loosely, giving him an appearance that might have been comical under other circumstances. Nevertheless, his proud nose and broad forehead were at once familiar to Alec, and he raised a hand in greeting.

The other figure stepped from behind the man then, and Alec was forced to surmise that it was Miss Landry. She did not look as he remembered her, but was far taller, and though bundled warmly, she appeared even at this distance to be in constant motion, as though to hold still would be to freeze on the spot. The restless energy was new since Alec had known her, though the bright, observant eyes were the same.

She spotted Alec and the others at once, and said something to the guard and her father before stepping briskly and decisively toward the prisoners, leaving the two men to trail behind.

She marched up to Alec and extended her warmly-gloved hand. "Your father sends his greetings, Alexander."

Alec was unsure what she expected of him, but he settled for formality. He bowed courteously over her hand and pressed his lips to the back of her fur-lined traveling glove before standing and addressing her. "I appreciate your willingness to come out here and help us attend to our neglected appearance. I hope that your ride here was not too difficult."

She waved a hand dismissively. "It is no more than the duty owed to an old friend and a true patriot of our cause." She looked sharply at Gad, who had given her a warning glance at her words.

Gad was particularly intolerant of talk of loyalty to the Crown, and the other prisoners had warned Alec against antagonizing him – but Miss Landry was both beyond Gad's jurisdiction and innocent of his strictures.

The guard broke eye contact with her and looked away, scowling. While there might be a price to pay later, Alec was heartened to see Gad humbled, if only by the tiniest amount.

Mister Landry caught up with his daughter then, a travel valise clutched in his hand. He nodded briskly to Alec, saying hurriedly, "So good to see you again, my boy," before turning to speak urgently with Miss Landry.

Though he spoke in an undertone, Alec could hear him clearly. "We'll have none of your high spirits now, Holly. We are here at the sufferance of these guards, and any offense we might give them will provide the excuse they need to force us to depart without doing what we came for."

Turning to Jonas, he said in a polite tone, "Might we pray the favor of a solid chair in which Miss Landry can ask the men to sit while she attends to them? It will make the work go much more quickly, as well as ease the strain on my daughter's arms as she works."

Jonas dispatched Gad to fetch a chair from the guardhouse with a wordless jerk of his chin, and then inclined his head graciously to Mister Landry. Opening the valise, Mister Landry beckoned the guard over.

"As you can see, these are but the ordinary tools of a barber, though I understand well enough that your safety requires they cannot be allowed to fall into the hands of prisoners. So as to avoid any possible suspicion of my daughter, I would invite you to observe her work closely, so that you may satisfy yourself that no item which might be useful to a prisoner passes from her to any of these men."

Jonas nodded, clearly satisfied, but Mister Landry continued. "Furthermore, I encourage you to take a count of all of these tools now, before she begins working, and perform a similar accounting when she is finished, to assure yourself that we leave with everything that we brought with us, save that we leave behind ourselves some measure of self-respect for these poor men."

As Jonas peered into the valise, Gad returned with a chair, setting it down before Miss Landry with a faint scowl.

She assessed the light and turned the seat slightly, and then said, "Alexander, will you sit?"

"Aye, Miss Landry." Alec took his seat and watched as Miss Landry unwound the muffler around her throat and removed her gloves.

Jonas completed his inspection of the valise, and Mister Landry handed it over to his daughter.

She set it on the ground and pulled out a wooden comb, which she set to work with on Alec's hair, untangling it in preparation for cutting. Her hands were gentle, though the comb still managed to find a few knotted snarls in his hair that required painful amounts of force to undo. Alec could hear Miss Landry tutting to herself under her breath as she worked through them, and it was a relief to them both when she at last was able to pass the comb through his hair without resistance.

"Have you any particular requests?" She stood behind him, the comb holding the hair clear of his neck.

Jonas called out to her, "Just cut it short enough to discourage such vermin as may appear in these conditions."

Alec felt a shudder run though her at the thought, and

grinned in spite of himself, glad that she could not see his face.

She said, testily, "Short you shall have it, then – short enough to wear a wig, were you a gentleman."

Alec felt himself color at her gibe and the implication that he was common and coarse. He sat in a prison not for some low crime, but for the offense of having taken up arms on the behalf of his sovereign. Should that not give him some status, even in the eyes of a plain-faced girl?

She said nothing further to insult him, though, and set to work efficiently, her shears slicing smoothly through his hair, her fingers cool against his exposed scalp as she moved.

He gazed at the view, the countryside beyond the walls of the prison laid out in the morning light. They were at a high point within the walls, and the low, bare hills of early spring had not yet taken on the vibrant green he knew they would erupt into in the coming weeks.

His hair fell in great, heavy hanks onto his shoulders and down his back, and the parts that fell past his face as Miss Landry worked around to the front of his head tickled his nose as they passed.

He raised a finger, and her hands drew away as she gave him a questioning look. He sneezed explosively, then lowered his hand again.

He heard her murmur under her breath, "Bless you," and he replied just as quietly, "Thank you."

She finished with the top of his head, and swept her hand over it, brushing away a few stray hairs. "Lean your head back, then, that I may get at your beard." Turning as he did her bidding, she called out to Gad, "Can you bring me some water, sir, in a bowl or a bucket?"

Gad sighed and trudged off, clearly unhappy at finding himself fetching and drawing for a girl of questionable sympathies.

While Gad worked at the well, Miss Landry used the shears to trim Alec's beard, getting it down to a length where her razor might be of some use. "I wish that we had the ability to work up a lather with some soap, but the trade from London being interrupted, I have not been able to lay hands on any in these parts, so we'll have to make do without it."

Alec answered honestly, "I've known no different in the militia, so do not let it worry you."

A breeze stirred, and Alec shivered slightly as the chill reached his scalp for the first time in months. Gad came back with a bucket holding a scant quart of cold water, but Miss Landry thanked him as though he'd fetched her a full barrel.

She drew the razor from her valise and dipped it in the water, saying quietly to Alec, "Hold still now."

He scowled. It wasn't as though this was the first time he'd had a shave, after all. However, he stayed very still as she drew the blade down his cheek, and did not even jump when she nicked him at the point of his jaw.

She muttered to herself, and if Alec did not know better, he would have thought that she had cursed. He could feel the warm trickle of blood as a stark contrast to the cold water that dripped from the razor as she dipped it again and shaved his other cheek, this time without incident.

Next, the cold steel swept over his chin, encountering little resistance as it severed hair. Though he felt no nick, he perceived another rivulet of warm blood trickling down from under his lip, and he could see Miss Landry biting her own lip in frustration.

"I'll do your moustache now, if you please."

Alec obediently pulled the skin taut, his upper lip wrapped absurdly over his teeth, and he couldn't help but take note of her thumb braced against his mouth as she carefully shaved under his nose and away toward herself.

"Lift your chin, please," she said, swirling the razor in the bucket to rinse it off. She laid the steel blade under the point of his chin and applied just a bit of pressure as she brought it down his neck smoothly. Though a couple of hairs pulled a bit before they parted, he felt no nicks with this pass, nor with the next.

With shorter, surer strokes, she finished the job, working around the edges of his face and neck to achieve a nice, even shave. She stood back and surveyed him, grimacing slightly to herself. Alec wondered what she saw as she looked him over, and whether she grimaced at her work or the man on whom she'd practiced.

She dispelled whatever doubts she'd had, though, and nodded briskly. "You'll do." She raised her voice and called out to the rest of the prisoners queued up. "Who's to be next?"

Alec stood, brushing fallen hair from his clothing.

The old thief Richard looked Alec over, and swallowed hard. "I suppose that would be me. I trust that you've got the feel for the razor now, and won't be taking chunks out of the rest of us?"

Alec looked up sharply at the thief's question, and shot back, "I'll take a chunk out of you, if you cannot keep a civil tongue in your mouth toward a gentlewoman who has come here to attend to your grooming."

The thief raised his hands. "I meant no insult by it. It's

only that I've got this brand on my cheek, and it takes some extra care to avoid catching it on a razor. Indeed, I've yet to find a barber who doesn't nick it at least once."

Miss Landry gave him a quick shake of her head. "I'll make no promises. I've little enough experience with shaving any man, let alone one with scars. Perhaps it would be more sensible to leave you with a beard trimmed like Mister Tinsworth's head?"

The thief pursed his mouth in thought for a moment, then nodded. "I can bear that," he said. "Though I've paid for a shave."

Jonas stepped up quickly, saying, "I will take care of that for you, Richard. Have your seat, and let the lady get on with her work."

Miss Landry appeared about to say something, but motioned the old thief into his place in the chair. Alec stepped back and returned to the group of other prisoners, watching her efficiently repeat the process of combing, cutting, and trimming Richard's hair. It seemed to him that her movements were more sure, and perhaps a touch less gentle with the thief than they had been for himself.

The rest of the men took their turns, emerging transformed – though in truth, Alec did not think that the transformation always did them any favors. One man, another of the common criminals among their number, turned out to have a wicked scar that wrapped nearly around his entire head, revealed when the hair concealing it was cut away.

At Alec's questioning stare when he returned to the group, the man said with a grin, "A Mohegan tried to scalp me, but I got a knife into his gut before he could finish the job."

Alec wasn't sure whether or not to believe him, but he nodded and turned away, unwilling to think further on whatever incident could so mark any man.

Before midday, Miss Landry was finished with the last of the prisoners, and had only drawn blood on two others, the very last men to go under her razor. After the second man had jumped and cursed aloud, she had stepped back, holding the blade clear of his movement. "The blade is dulled with use, I am afraid, and you must be even more still than your fellows, if I am not to cut you again."

The prisoner had scowled, but had turned his bleeding cheek back toward her to let her finish the job. Alec thought he could see her hand shaking a bit as she lowered the blade to his skin, but her stroke was steady and sure.

She stood up straight after she had finished, her hand kneading the small of her back.

Jonas and Mister Landry shook hands, and Alec saw Jonas hand Miss Landry's father a slip of paper, which the older man tucked into his waistcoat with a small, grim smile of satisfaction. "Come, my dear," he called out to his daughter.

Turning to Alec, he said, "I will carry your greetings back to your father, and hope that we may be welcome here again when next your company needs grooming."

Jonas interjected, "I am sure that she will find a ready supply of customers at that time, once they have a chance to see the fine work that she did on the brave fellows who took her up on her offer this time."

Miss Landry answered, "Aye, and perhaps they'll even pay a better price the next time." Both Jonas and her father seemed to be discomfited at her comment, but she laughed gaily.

Her smile transformed her face, and for the first time, Alec saw her as other men must see her, rather than as the girl he'd known for years already.

Long after she and her father left, as he labored at the forge, he thought on the peculiar effect that the momentary smile had had on the girl's face, and wondered how he could ensure that both she and her smile returned soon.

Chapter 8

By sundown, a cold rain was falling, and Alec wished for any kind of hat to shield his head from the chill and stop the rain from running down his neck and under his shirt. Perhaps not a cocked hat – it wouldn't do to let anyone think that his loyalty to the Crown could be overthrown by so small a matter as physical comfort – but some sort of broad-brimmed sailor's hat wouldn't go amiss.

While the downpour was not so heavy or constant as the wet that Alec imagined assaulted men on the deck of a ship in foul weather, it was enough to encourage a cough by the next day. As he hacked and spat in the darkness, he could tell that it was still raining aboveground.

What had been no more than an occasional drip of water now sounded like a small, energetic brook, babbling and chuckling as it coursed past the bunks and down into the depths of the unused parts of the mine. Alec shivered and drew his thin blanket tighter about himself. He had no enthusiasm for the morning meal that day, so he shoveled the cold mush of peas down more out of habit than hunger.

Now, as he awaited his shift at the forge, he found himself hoping that its heat would warm him through, while he prayed that the smoke from the charcoal would not aggravate the cough that wouldn't release him. Just the thought of the vapor sent him into another hacking, choking fit. As he spat again, he tasted blood, and he wondered at it, worried that it might portend worse to come.

Nonetheless, he forced himself to climb the ladder out of the black gloom underground, and into a clinging, sodden, grey version of the same. At the forge, he could strike only a few blows between coughing fits, and his rate of production was so pitiful that Gad stormed over to scold him.

"You get your hair cut, and suddenly you fancy yourself a proper gentleman, do you, too good to labor like the rest of us? You'd best do better tomorrow, else I'll put the lash to you, just see if I don't." Turning to walk away, Gad muttered almost more to himself than to Alec, "The lot of you what got your barbering done yesterday have been slacking today, whining about one sort of malady or another."

He whirled back around to Alec, waving a finger under the prisoner's nose so closely that Alec could smell the fish the man had eaten for lunch. "If this is some plot by you wasters to try to persuade us to increase your rations or reduce your work, you may be assured that none of us will have any tolerance whatever for it. You've a quota to fill, and you'll work until you've filled it."

However, the overcast sky and the waning light of the sun setting somewhere behind the clouds conspired to make it too dark to work at an earlier hour than usual. Despite the lengthening days of the advancing spring, the caprices of weather dictated that there was little point in continuing long before he'd met the mark in the barrel of nails that he was supposed to be filling.

Jonas came around to send him down below, and glanced into the barrel, merely shaking his head. "I hope that you weren't so consumed today with thoughts of that girl that it hindered your production."

Alec shook his head violently, the motion triggering yet another spasm of coughing. It went on and on, stealing his breath away entirely, and refusing to loose its hold. He saw darkness close in on him and felt himself falling, spinning into merciful oblivion.

When he returned to consciousness, he was inside the guardhouse, on one of the guards' bunks. He struggled to raise himself to a sitting position, but Jonas' gentle hands pushed him back down onto the bunk.

"Just give yourself a moment to catch your breath, lad. You gave us a bad moment there – thought that Gad was going to turn out to be right, and we'd be spending the night digging a grave for you."

Alec had enough energy to look around for Gad and shoot the guard a glare. Gad shrugged and looked away, uncaring. Jonas put the back of his hand to Alec's forehead, and the gesture took Alec back to his childhood, when his mother would do the same whenever he fell ill, her expression concealing, as did Jonas', the worry that he was afflicted with a fever that might take him away entirely.

He recalled that she had told him and his brothers stories of her own childhood, when she had watched a brother and three sisters all get taken by a fever over the course of a single fortnight. Whatever it had been, it had bypassed her entirely, but had left her to care for her baby sister, as it soon took her mother as well. How ironic, then, that it was a fever that had taken her in the end, reuniting her with not only her sons, but the rest of those she had lost.

The thought of how his father would react to news that his last remaining son was ill gave him a new determination to overcome this, whatever it was, with whatever he had left to give.

Jonas shook his head, concern etched on his face. "Seems that you fellows who got your hair trimmed to my instructions yesterday all had need of it to help preserve your health. Ought to call you lot Sampson's Squad or some such, eh?" He muttered, "Weakened by the loss of your hair, who would have thought it."

Addressing Alec again, Jonas said, "All right, you, let's see if you can bring yourself to the ladder and make your way down without fainting dead away and dropping to your death."

Alec nodded and sat up gingerly, and then stood. He did not feel at all faint, just bone-weary, but that was normal at the end of days spent at the forge. "I believe that I can get myself down," he said with more conviction than he felt.

Jonas nodded and jerked his head toward the iron door in the next room. "Get gone with you, then. I'll look for you to be hale and ready in the morning, and will want a report from Thomas as to your condition, and that of the others who gave up their hair yesterday. Pass the word to him of that."

"Aye, sir," said Alec, and as he approached the iron door, Gad swung it open with a malevolent leer.

"Tomorrow's another day," he said, too quietly for Jonas to hear. "Might yet collect on the lottery we are taking up here against the odds of which of you will fall next."

Alec ignored him pointedly and started down the ladder.

"Had me hopes up when you fainted, but you turned out to just be another Tory what melts like a snowflake under hot breath. Here's to you melting away in good time, Tory." Gad touched his knuckle to his forehead in a mocking salute, and swung the door shut before Alec could answer in any way.

By the time he reached the bottom, he was shaking with exhaustion, and he bypassed the tables where Thomas was holding forth, heading straight to his bunk. He noted that he was not the only one eschewing the dinner table, and his brow furrowed at Jonas' comment.

He dimly remembered the story of Sampson's hair, but could not recall its loss having caused any sort of illness, only weakness in battle. Unlike the wily Delilah, though, Alec had no suspicion at all that Miss Landry had done anything purposeful to weaken the prisoners.

Indeed, it seemed entirely clear that her purpose was to strengthen them, to rescue their humanity from their descent into bestial appearance, not to unman them as Delilah had crippled Sampson. Furthermore, Alec remembered regarding the story of Sampson's strength deriving from his hair as somewhat ludicrous when he'd first learned it.

A man's strength in battle was not determined by the length of his hair, but by his force of will, and the power he was able to direct into his muscles and sinews. Alec had never felt that he was particularly well-suited for the sort of combat he had volunteered to face; he was driven to it by a sense of duty, both to his lost brothers and to his family's loyalty to the King.

He supposed, as he shivered well beyond what was justified by the steady, damp chill of the mine, that this was another sort of battle, and he hoped fervently that he was better equipped to fight this one than he had turned out to be for the hazards of military service.

Chapter 9

Alec did not sleep well that night. Whether it was his own ceaseless cough, or those of the other prisoners, there was no peace for anyone in the dank chamber of the mine. The worst part of it was not knowing how far into the night they had endured. The only thing that gave evidence of the passage of time was the retreat of the rivulet through their space, back to a steady dripping, as the rains exhausted themselves aboveground.

It was almost a relief when Gad shouted down and raised his customary clangor with pots and pans at the top of the mine shaft. Most mornings when it was his duty to rouse the prisoners, they cursed and shouted insults up the shaft, as he seemed to take a particular delight in tormenting them before sending down their food.

Today, though, the men roused themselves groggily from their bunks, which set up new paroxysms of coughing from several corners of the chamber. One of the men groaned and called out, "Old Richard's gone and copped it during the night."

As the prisoners pressed forward to examine the old thief's still form, Alec had to suppress the thought that this would cost Gad his lottery, and struggled to keep his face from showing the tiny jolt of joy that thought gave him.

Richard had been a taciturn fellow at best, and his history of thievery on the outside made men here regard him with a certain level of distrust. As a result, he was not among the better-liked men of their company.

Still, nobody liked to see death, no matter what opportunities it presented. In Richard's case, his shoes had been traded for someone else's, and his blanket spirited away before Gad was summoned to examine his corpse.

Thomas called up the shaft to their jailer, "We lost another over the night, sir. Should you like to come down and inspect the body?"

Gad muttered a curse loudly enough to be heard at the base of the ladder as he started down its rungs, and asked, "Which of you lot was it this time?"

"Old Richard," Thomas replied, and Gad cursed with more feeling now as he reached the end of the ladder.

As he passed by, Alec could hear Gad muttering, "The old thief managed to rob me this time," as the guard shot Alec a baleful glare. He came to face the cold corpse, still stretched on his bunk. He raised the man's arm, let it drop with a dull thud onto the wood, and said, "All right, then, let's get him up top and detail grave diggers." He sighed, "I don't suppose that we'll make quota today, either."

Alec wasn't clear on where this quota had come from, only that after a few days of practice at the art, the guards had told them how much they were to produce each day, and threatened to cut rations for any shift that fell short. So far, that threat had been an empty one – Alec suspected that it was because there was enough money coming in from being able to sell nails to a market hungry for locally-made replacements for the interrupted imports from trade abroad.

"Choose from among those who are not sick – there's no need to send additional men to their graves, or to make the rest of you dig more graves than you already must."

"Aye, sir," Thomas said, frowning. He turned to regard the prisoners. "Edward, Phillip, George, you three help me get Richard up the ladder, and then we'll figure out who is best suited for digging a grave today."

Thomas grimaced as another man began coughing. "Gad, you had best send for someone to physic us, too, lest we be forced to dig a lot more graves."

Gad looked at him sharply. "Perhaps you stick to keeping your men in line, and leave their care and feeding to those who have the responsibility, prisoner."

Thomas did not argue, but merely bowed, in a sketch of the respect that he would have demonstrated for nearly any of the other guards.

Gad returned to the mine shaft and went up the ladder, muttering to himself all the way.

When the guard was safely out of earshot, Thomas said quietly, "If the day comes that our fortunes change to permit it, Gad will be the first against the wall to pay for his role in keeping us just well enough to work, and for his contempt for us while we were under his power."

Alec pretended that he hadn't heard Thomas' declaration. He had the sense that it was not safe to speculate on the possibility of revenge against their jailers, and that to do so could jeopardize their already precarious position in the prison.

In another moment, his philosophical considerations were set aside for yet another round of the hacking cough, which he heard from several others, as well. The men Thomas had detailed were getting to the grim work of moving Richard to the mine shaft, where the litter was already bumping its way down to carry the corpse up.

In relatively short order, Alec stood with the other men around the grave, dug just deep enough, and no longer than was needed. The rains had turned the soil heavy and sullen under the prisoners' shovels, and though the sky was clear today, a chill breeze blew across the jailyard. Jonas had decided to keep everyone belowground for the rest of the day, if only to avoid exposing the guards to whatever contagion seemed to be spreading through the prisoners.

So far, the cough still only afflicted those who had sat for haircuts, but none of them had shown any signs of it letting up. Alec had seen Clem blowing his nose, though he had not surrendered his hair to Miss Landry's shears. It seemed only a matter of time before everyone was sick, and the guards wanted no part of it.

As the day wore on in the darkness, Alec found himself overcome with a shivering chill, and he was unsurprised when Thomas pronounced him fevered. Before dinnertime, two other men who'd been coughing were fighting fevers as well, and Clem had begun coughing now, too.

Thomas had those who were sick move to the bunks at the furthest end of the chamber, and set up charcoal burners around them, both to improve the air and to lend some warmth to the men. Those who still appeared healthy stayed up toward the mine shaft, and other than Thomas, they stayed away, lest they should also become afflicted.

After another endless night of fitful sleep, Alec felt the fever's heat in his eyelids retreat, and while the cough still seized him at all hours, he thought that he could safely say that he was feeling better this morning than he had the last.

Not all were so fortunate, however, and those who were still well had two more graves to dig that day. Alec dully stood by each of the holes in the ground, watching men he'd come to know being lowered into their rough graves. He couldn't help but wonder whether he would ever leave these grounds, or if he would also find a final resting place within the walls of the prison.

Jonas had sought advice from a doctor, and the man had expressed the opinion that though there was little point in trying to physic the sufferers individually, it seemed likely to him that the close air in the mine was promoting their phlegmatic humors, and so he urged Jonas to encourage even the sick men to spend as much time as practical out of doors.

As a result, Jonas had those who were well enough back at the forges, and the rest were being led about the grounds in a procession. It would have been comical but for the occasional pauses to let one of their number recover from a coughing fit.

One of these pauses ended with Clem laid out flat on the ground in what Alec presumed was a faint not unlike the one he'd suffered himself. It was only when Jonas was summoned, and he in turn summoned Thomas and a fresh crew of gravediggers, that Alec understood that the gangly youth would never rise again.

He felt a stab of sadness at this fresh loss. He had come to know Clem as they'd labored together at the forge, and though the boy was made of more ambition than ability, Alec had developed a degree of admiration for his proclivity to see the good in most anything that happened.

Though the advent of nail-making had relegated him to simple tasks that required no great strength, Clem had been a close observer of the tasks he was not asked to undertake, and had been eager to try his hand at them, no matter how hopeless it was that he would actually be able to perform them.

He'd spoken of a sister and father who both depended upon the pittance he sent home – he was one who had missed the opportunity for a haircut out of frugality, though he'd hardly needed the shave in any case – and Alec wondered suddenly who might send word to them that their brother and son had been felled by disease.

Jonas stood by where Clem's body lay, a grim expression on his face, and Alec approached him.

"Sir, I have a question for you."

Jonas grunted noncommittally, which Alec took to mean that he could continue.

"Sir, when a prisoner dies, do you undertake to inform our families?"

Jonas scowled without look at Alec, evidently unhappy at the chore that the question had reminded him still lay ahead. All he said, though, was, "Aye, I do."

"And if you cannot locate our family?"

Jonas looked at Alec now. "I know where your father can be reached, if that's what concerns you, lad."

Alec held up a hand in negation. "Nay, not at all – indeed, I feel that I am on the mend now – but I wondered about poor Clem."

Jonas' expression returned to one of grim contemplation. "Aye, I know where to reach his father, and though I cannot give him a body to bury, I can at least give him the peace of mind of knowing that his son is no longer in bondage – either behind these walls with you lot, or on earth with us all."

Chapter 10

The wave of illness that had swept through the prisoners following Miss Landry's visit had not touched the guards, and after Clem was lowered into the ground, the affliction seemed to recede into the normal sort of sniffles and coughs that a group of men exposed to hard labor and cold weather were subject to in normal times.

While the other graves were unmarked mounds, Alec prevailed upon Jonas to write Clem's name and dates down clear, and took it upon himself to painstakingly scratch "Clemson Gates, 1762-1781" into a piece of wood he'd scrounged from the scraps remaining from the fence construction the prior year. He hammered it into the ground, feeling that it was a wholly inadequate memorial for a life that had burned with promise, but had, ultimately, burned out instead.

Gad looked on with an expression of detached tolerance, and when Alec finished placing the makeshift marker, the guard hooked a thumb toward the forge where Alec was due to begin work. "If you're done with your sentimentality, your team is waiting for you."

Alec glared at him, but said nothing, stalking to his place at the forge.

In Clem's place at the packing station, stirring a pot of lazily bubbling, rendered lard, was Patrick, a grim, compact militiaman, captured just before Clem had been.

He nodded briskly at Alec, his normally taciturn expression softened with a touch of compassion. He spoke quietly. "'Twas a decent thing you done, boy. Clem would have liked it."

"Thank you, Patrick." Alec nodded to Thomas, who stood ready by the bellows, and bent to retrieve both his hammer and the iron stock from the ground where they sat.

Losing himself in the labor of making nails, Alec was surprised when Thomas raised a hand to signal that it was time for their shift to end. He had only had to pause to cough a few times in the hours of mindless work, and though he'd felt weaker than a fresh-weaned kitten the prior day, his strength seemed to be back today.

Glancing over into the barrel of nails, he was surprised again to see that they'd exceeded the mark Jonas had scratched into the inside of it, hiding the scar in the wood under a jumble of finished nails.

One less thing for Gad to harass them about, Alec figured, but he otherwise felt no particular joy in the accomplishment. Instead, he turned away and trudged wearily back toward the guardhouse, ready for the blessed intercession of sleep to dull the ache in his chest.

While some of it was likely from the lingering effects of his illness, he knew that some of it was from the loss of his – well, friends was probably too strong a word, but they were more than merely fellow prisoners of circumstance. They were men he'd shared meals with, who'd struggled with the same troubles and frustrations, and some of whom had helped ease the long days of their confinement with stories and even just idle chatter.

Before Alec could pass through the guardhouse to begin his trip back underground to the prison chamber, Jonas flagged him over to his desk by the front door of the guards' room, a folded sheet of paper held in his hand.

Alec approached, and Jonas extended the paper to him.

"Letter to you from your father," he said by way of explanation.

Alec accepted it, but stood turning it over in his hands helplessly for a moment before Jonas looked up at him.

"Can you not read it, I suppose?"

Alec shook his head, shamefaced. "I... I was supposed to have a tutor before my brothers died and I joined the militia," he said, but Jonas raised his hand and shook his head to cut him off.

"It matters not. If you would like, I can read it aloud to you; I've read it already to ensure that it contains nothing of intrigues to mutiny against our guard or otherwise defy the authority of the Committee of Safety, so you'll be entrusting no secrets to me that I do not already possess."

Alec frowned, but handed the letter back to Jonas. "I'd be much obliged, sir."

Jonas nodded and flipped the page open. "Dear Son," he began. "I have had a report from Miss Landry of your good health and the general conduct of the men with whom you serve in bondage. I am gratified to learn that several of your fellows were able to avail themselves of Miss Landry's services, and thereby improve themselves, if only in the short term."

Jonas snorted in spite of himself and looked up from the page to address Alec. "'Twill take more than a haircut and a shave to improve you lot, but I suppose it makes you somewhat easier to look upon, so I'll grant him that argument."

Alec forced himself to smile in reply, as little as he liked being made sport of, and Jonas looked back down to the page.

"I am sorry to report that upon her return hither, Miss Landry was taken ill with a fever, but it has thankfully passed without dire consequence. She is, of course, of a strong constitution, and her generally rugged good health has served her well in her recovery. I mention it only in hope that she was not exposed to whatever contagion afflicted her in the bad air of the prison, which I imagine must be greatly damaging of the warmer humors. However, if I grasp the advice of the most learned of philosophers, then the exposure you have to the fires of the forges must balance that air and maintain you. Miss Landry not having the benefit of your time before the fire was sickened as a result, but she remains willing, nay, eager, to return and offer her assistance to you and those of your fellows as shall desire it, to maintain your appearances as gentlemen of the Crown."

Jonas looked up grimly at Alec. "I was tempted to censor that part for disloyalty to our state of Connecticut, but decided that it was likely you already have had sufficient opportunity to reflect upon the error of your ways and the flaws in his suppositions, without needing me to prevent you from being exposed to them."

Returning to the letter, Jonas read, "Mister Landry, having passed his time well away from the bad air of the mine, was not taken ill, and will supervise any future visit with his daughter to ensure that she is placed well away from its fell influence. I do trust that you found her visit pleasant, and warmly hope that you will consider spending the time to come to better know her worthy qualities for so long as you may be confined there. You are of an age and a condition where a partnership with someone from a family as respectable as hers would not go amiss. If I speak out of turn, please forgive me, but my advanced age and the reverses of the past years have me eager to grasp for any spark of potential joy that presents itself to me. I close with warm hopes for your swift liberation, and for an end to this miserable war as quickly as can be managed. Your devoted father, Philip Tinsworth, et cetera, et cetera."

Jonas smiled at Alec and handed him the letter, which Alec folded and tucked into the pocket of his breeches. "Well, I must say that I am sorrowed to hear that Miss Landry was taken ill in the same way that you fellows were, but she seems a spirited and likely enough lass. Should you like me to take down a reply letter to your father?"

Alec stammered, "I-I think I should like to, yes, but I would like a moment to consider what to say, if I may?"

Jonas nodded. "Certainly. But don't take too long – I think that Gad is already sending down the evening ration, and I don't know whether the others will save anything for you in your absence." Alec felt certain that Thomas would keep his share aside for him, at least to the extent that he could, but took the guard's meaning clearly.

"Very well, sir. I will draft a reply just as soon as you are ready to take it down."

"Good lad. I'll go and get my pen, and what paper I can spare."

Alec thought about what to say while he waited, and was ready when Jonas returned from fetching pen and paper from the chest by what must have been his bunk.

The guard set himself up to write, looking up expectantly

at him.

Alec nodded and began, speaking slowly enough to let Jonas catch up after every few words.

"My dear father, I am sorry to say that we, too, were visited by a bout with some affliction that started with a cough, and in some cases, proceeded to a fever. I am sorry to relate that despite the energetic efforts of our guards"— Jonas looked up and crooked an eyebrow at him, but he pressed on—"we lost three men from among the prisoners, including one whom I considered a friend. For my own part, I weathered the illness with no more than moderate difficulty, and am now well on the way to the full restoration of my faculties. As for the matter of considering the pursuit of Miss Landry's hand from behind the bars of a prison, I must confess that I find the idea somewhat preposterous to think of at this moment. I can offer her naught but the likelihood of an absent husband, and one worn into uselessness by the hazards of hard service, for the foreseeable span of years. While all may hope for a swift end to the present troubles between these colonies"—Jonas frowned, but kept writing—"and our sovereign, those hopes have been dashed for all of these past five years and more, and so I cannot contemplate asking Miss Landry, nor any woman, no matter how worthy, to consider seriously any suit I might make for her hand. Pray, do not permit this to reach her ears as any reflection upon her qualities, which are, as you note, many and worthy, but only as a sober consideration of what may be best for her interests. I am, sir, your obedient son, Alexander Tinsworth, et cetera, et cetera."

When Jonas' pen had stopped scratching, he looked over the letter, and commented dryly, "The bit about our 'energetic efforts' on the behalf of you prisoners was, perhaps, laying it on a bit thick, my boy, but there's no harm in that, I suppose. I changed your comment calling our states 'colonies,' though, to read, 'these united States and the British crown,' in keeping with the style of correspondence penned by those not imprisoned for taking up arms against your countrymen."

Alec grimaced but nodded. "As you must; I cannot complain, since you have so kindly transcribed my words for me."

He paused, and Jonas waved him in the direction of the kitchen, where the iron door leading underground still stood open. "Go and join your fellows, and eat whatever they may have left for you. I'll dispatch your letter by the next post and levy a charge against your account, and advise you whenever there may be a reply."

Alec bowed slightly, then hurried through the kitchen and started down the ladder.

Chapter 11

Alec slipped his shoes off gratefully and set them down beside him on his narrow bunk, eager to let his feet dry under the blanket as he slept. He tucked the thin fabric under his heels and pulled the other end up as close to his chin as he could manage, to conserve what body heat he could.

Around him in the close and smoky darkness, he could hear men coughing and shifting around, trying just as he was to get comfortable enough to settle down for the night. As weary as he was, he thought he should be able to escape into sleep readily, but his father's words kept coming back to stalk his thoughts, and left him wondering whether he was guilty of the sin of hubris.

If Miss Landry was willing – as his father seemed to imply she was – who was he to deny her what satisfaction she could get from a match to a prisoner of the rebellion? Left unstated in his reply was possibility, remote as it now seemed, that the contest between the American rebels and the forces loyal to the Crown would come to a favorable end, improving his fortunes as well, and the Landry family's position.

Were that to happen, would he not be more than just a suitable match, but one actually desirable to a fellow Loyalist? And if so, what did it matter that she was relatively plain? He had to admit that he did not remember her plainness when he thought of her smile, and it was even possible that she was left plain primarily because of the difficulties under which she and her father labored due to the convulsions of war.

In happier circumstances, was it not possible that both her good fortune and her general happiness with her place in the world would make her more pleasing, both to the eye and to the heart of a true patriot of the British sovereign?

He was remembering, with no small happiness, how gentle her hands had been on his face as she'd shaved and barbered him, when he heard a nearly silent rustling, followed by the clear ring of metal on stone right by his ear, and a muffled curse.

Instinctively, his hand shot out, and he found himself clutching a struggling arm in his fingers.

A voice rasped by his ear, low and whining, "Geroff me, I didn't mean anything by it, your shoes stand by you as before, and no harm done."

Alec recognized the voice of one of the few remaining common criminals among their number, a grey and quiet man whose crimes were unspecified, but which appeared to include thievery.

He hissed into the darkness, his grip steady and firm. "Daniel, isn't it? What business have you with my few possessions?"

Alec felt rather than heard the man's vigorous nod. "Aye, 'tis me, Daniel. I would never have done aught with your shoes, except that old William had told me that I should have them, if he happened to cop it whilst we were still here. Then when he did cop it, you showed up wearing them, and I never did have a chance to make good on his bequest."

Alec's hold on the man's arm became gentler as he thought over his claim.

It was true that he'd taken possession of the shoes in a fairly irregular manner, and that none were given a chance to state any prior claim before the deed was done. Thomas had encouraged him in the matter, though, and he had thought little of it since that day.

"Have you any witness to your claim?"

Again, he could feel Daniel's head shake sadly from side to side, rather than being able to perceive it with his eyes, dark-adapted though they might be.

"Nay, only old Richard, and none believed any witness he bore for anything, so oft he did or said whatever he thought might give him some advantage, so I did not think to press the matter, but had hoped to simply accomplish by stealth what I could not by wit."

Alec could not help but admire Daniel's forthrightness about his dishonesty, and could not argue his point about old Richard's reputation. As he pondered, he heard a metallic scrape from the floor, and was reminded of the ringing sound that had alerted him to the attempted theft in the first place.

He realized that it was the coin that William had secreted in the toe of one shoe that had fallen to the ground, and with a fresh burst of admiration for Daniel's boldness, he released the man's arm, leapt from the bunk, and crouched to the ground, his hand casting out to find the thief's foot atop the coin, his toes curled around it, trying to secure it even without the use of his hands.

He struck at Daniel's foot blindly, eliciting a hissed curse from the man, but gaining the coin from the floor.

Daniel jumped back, whining, "You've gone and lamed me now, and for what?"

"Perhaps we should speak to Thomas of this in the morning," Alec said, then added maliciously, "Or might Jonas be interested to hear that you are back to your old habits, even among our wretched company?"

He knew he'd struck a sensitive point when Daniel mewled, "No, no need, my foot will be fine, and I only wish that you had let me return your rightful property that I so carelessly knocked to the floor. You understand, don't you, that I'd no intention to keep it, but was going to leave it in the shoes that I replaced William's with, from my own feet. Surely, you don't mean to expose me to the lash over a simple misunderstanding?"

It was as Alec had thought – Daniel must have as long a record of thievery as Richard had, if he feared the lash for something as minor as stealing from another prisoner.

Alec smiled grimly into the darkness. "Leave me my shoes, then, and do not disturb my property or my sleep again, and there will be no need to tell anyone of what has passed this night. I am sorry that your claim to William's shoes could not be made in better faith, but let us consider the matter settled, and speak no more of it."

He considered for a long moment, and then added, "Your hand, Daniel, if you would."

Daniel's hand brushed against his own, groping blindly in the darkness, and Alec took it, turned it palm up, and placed the coin in it. "Take this as a token of my regret at having interfered with your bequest, and may you find better use for it than I have."

He felt Daniel's hand close over the coin slowly, as though disbelieving that the gesture was real. The other man started to simper his gratitude, but Alec stopped him, taking the outstretched hand in his again.

Wrapping both of his own hands over the thief's and firmly closing Daniel's fingers over the coin, he added, "Let me not catch you at my shoes again, though, nor any other man's property, or I shall have to bear witness of your acts this night."

"Aye, sir, and thank you. I'll give you no cause to regret the kindness you've shown me."

Alec doubted that, but released the man's hand from his own and climbed back into his bunk to stare into the darkness as he listened to the furtive sounds of the criminal returning to his own bunk. He wondered whether the precious possession — first stolen, then recovered and granted as a gift — would really do the man any good, or whether it would simply serve to teach him that the ways of deceit and theft could benefit him.

Alec was still pondering the question as sleep finally overtook him and carried him off into the dark and quiet night.

Chapter 12

Within the span of just a couple of days, the weather had turned from cold, torrential rain, to one of the sweetest periods of sunny springtime warmth that Alec could remember. His work before the forge was still heavy labor, and he was recovering no faster than any of the other sick men from his cough, but for the first time since his brothers' deaths, he found himself actually enjoying a day spent in the sun.

Daniel was no less servile in the daylight, insisting on taking over Alec's barrel loading. Patrick shrugged at the criminal's pleading expression. "If you want the work so badly, it's no loss to me. Jonas has wanted to shift me over to moving the iron stock anyway."

Alec gave the departing militiaman a bemused frown, but nodded to him and said, "All right, then, Daniel. I trust that you know your duties well enough?"

Daniel bobbed his head as eagerly as a fresh recruit at quartermaster offering an extra ration. "Oh, aye, sir, that I do. I'm to ensure that the nails are sealed against the damp by means of a bit of melted lard, and then to ensure that they are packed neatly and evenly in the barrels."

"Just so," Alec said, and motioned him into place at his station beside the barrel. He set to his task, and noted with grudging respect that Daniel was actually doing a very careful job. After a while, he forgot to worry any further about it, as he settled into the mindless rote of shaping nail after nail from the iron stock.

By the time his shift was through, Daniel's steady, reliable movements seemed little more than an extension of Alec's own actions, though his ingratiating smile whenever he caught Alec's eye was off-putting. As they walked away from the forge at Jonas' call, Alec thought that the coin he'd handed over to Daniel might have been the cheapest purchase of devotion in history, and wondered how long it would last.

As they headed toward the guardhouse, Jonas motioned Alec over to him. "You've another letter," he said without preamble, and produced the folded sheet of paper. "If you'd like me to read it to you, I have time now to do it."

"Yes, sir, that would be too kind, thank you." Alec hated to hear an echo of Daniel's tone in his own voice, but he could not avoid the fact that the guard was kinder to him than his position required, and was by far the most humane of the jailers at the prison.

Alec reminded himself that he was, nonetheless, still his jailer.

Jonas led Alec to his desk again, and unfolded the page.

"Dear son. I have received your letter with both considerable pleasure and no small amount of surprise, until I realized that someone among the guards at the prison must have taken it down for you. Please convey to that man my gratitude, even as I tell you that it remains my fondest hope that we shall be able to resume your interrupted education before too many more months have passed. I am sorrowed to read that your company suffered illness and loss as a result of the same affliction that struck Miss Landry. I trust that you will be restored to complete health through the industry of your guards and fellow prisoners. As to that worthy Miss Landry, I esteem your position in the matter regarding a match between you and her, even as I respectfully differ. Your prospects, even should the current contest resolve unfavorably, are no worse than any other whom she might consider, and under certain circumstances, could indeed develop to be substantially better than she might elsewhere find. I do urge you to give the question fuller consideration, and I hope that we can engage in a frank discussion on it when I visit you next. Please reply by return post upon consultation with the guard at your prison, and tell me when I might be able to journey thence and pay you another visit. Your cousins send their greetings, and continue to be only too kind as my hosts, even as they keep their toes behind the plank laid down by our restive American friends, avoiding controversy at all costs and remaining in the good graces of the many committees that abound in these troubled days. I am your devoted father, Phillip Tinsworth, et cetera."

Jonas looked up from the page at Alec with an expectant expression.

Alec carefully kept his reaction off his face, but inside, he was struggling with a half-dozen conflicting urges. He settled for bowing slightly to Jonas and saying, "Please accept my father's thanks and mine for your assistance in our correspondence. I shall need some time before I can give him a reply, however. Can you advise me as to what I may tell him regarding another visit?"

Jonas appeared slightly disappointed at Alec's lack of response, but shrugged. "Most anytime is fine, on condition of good behavior and production in the nail-making industry."

"Of course," Alec replied, puzzled. "I would take those as understood, regardless." He put out his hand for the letter, and

Jonas folded it back up, tapping it smartly into Alec's open palm, smiling at his prisoner.

"Don't wait too long to reply," Jonas said, "I shouldn't like for your father to presume that we are standing between you."

Alec said nothing, merely bowed again, as though he wore a regimental coat and a sword at his waist, rather than the rags of a prisoner, and Jonas dismissed him with a tilt of his head.

Before Alec reached the iron door, however, there was a commotion outside, and Jonas leapt for the door, alarmed at any disruption to the routine of the prison.

The sudden urgency of his movement left Alec wondering if there was some cause for concern, some intelligence he had received that made him think that trouble might be brewing. Taken together with Jonas' strange warning about good behavior, Alec found that his heart was racing as he paused at the door to the mine shaft, waiting to see whether he might learn what the disturbance was.

In a few moments, his curiosity was rewarded, as Jonas and Gad let in three other men, all of whom looked miserable, and what remained of their militia uniforms in such poor repair that Alec couldn't tell whether they were officers or private soldiers.

Gad saw Alec in the kitchen and snapped, "Return at once to your barracks, prisoner. You were dismissed from your labors over a quarter of an hour ago – are you trying to earn a spell on the post?"

Jonas put a hand on Gad's arm, as though restraining him. "Nay, Gad, I just left Alec here considering a reply to his correspondence of this morning." Jonas shot Alec a look, though, and added, "We'll need to attend to that later on, though, boy; you'd best be heading down below ground, as Gad has instructed."

"Aye, sir," Alec answered quickly, and ducked through the iron door, his feet and hands finding the familiar ladder down.

He heard Gad curse under his breath as the guard banged the door closed and shot the bolt, locking Alec below with the other men.

In the chamber underground, Alec waited for his eyes to adjust as well as they would, and then made his way to Thomas.

"Looks like we may be joined by some new prisoners," he reported.

"Oh, yes? I'll wager that you're clinging to the hope that you'll no longer be the greenest member of our company, then."

The other men around the table laughed, and Alec smiled. "Aye, I'll not deny that it will be a relief to have some about who know less about life in this place than do I."

Thomas chuckled, his grin not quite visible through the gloom. "Now, I wouldn't go making any assumptions, lad. We've seen prisoners come and prisoners go, without they are ever cast down here into the darkness with us. It'll depend upon their status and their rank, as you know. No officer would ever be housed as we are, nor any member of the King's own men."

He laughed quietly to himself again, adding, "Well, except for Mister Miller, but who knows what circumstances might have provoked his dispatch to spend some time with the likes of us?" Another hoarse grunt of a laugh punctuated his comment. "Nay, this fate is reserved for none but the petty criminals and the loyal volunteers for the sake of the crown."

"Aye, and a dirty job it is, too, being classed with you lot," came a surly growl from the darkness.

Thomas asked, without rancor, "Who said that? There'll

be no rations for you in the morning, you filthy patriot criminal."

Alec said nothing, but thought he had recognized Daniel's voice, though it was hard to say, as he was more accustomed to hearing it spoken with either a whining or an obsequious tone.

Thomas waited a moment for his heckler to identify himself, and then continued, muttering under his breath, "To have to put up with abuse from the likes of him…" In a normal tone, he said to Alec, "Once we hear a man coming down the ladder, then you'll know that you're a rung or two above him, but even without them, you're a few steps ahead of our criminal element, no matter how long they've rotted in this hole."

His heckler responded with a loud, throat-clearing spit, and Thomas responded, "The lot of you can all go hungry tomorrow morning, if you should like."

The brewing argument was forestalled by the clang of iron from the top of the mine shaft as the door was flung open. At the sounds of Gad exhorting men to climb down faster, Alec felt nothing but compassion for the new prisoners.

"Looks like you'll be getting what you hoped for," Thomas snickered to him, but Alec couldn't bring himself to feel any satisfaction at the development, if it came at the expense of another man.

He heard the first of the new prisoners shout out in surprise and then yelp in pain as he fell from the bottom of the ladder, as Alec had himself not too long ago, and the rough laughter from the other men made him realize that his position among them was likely to remain one of an outsider, regardless of how many men joined them in bondage after him.

Chapter 13

The new prisoners were hard men, the sort who would cheerfully burn a settlement to the ground to ensure the demise of a single rebel hidden within its walls. Once they had recovered after the arranged indignity of their arrival belowground, they had moved with swift self-assurance to establish themselves as a group apart.

Thomas seemed confused at first by their lack of deference to him, but once he'd let them know what their sleeping arrangements would be, he left the newcomers to themselves.

They weren't interested in introductions, the gruffest of them saying only, "We don't expect to be here long enough to get to know any of you."

Thomas raised an eyebrow at the man. "Oh?"

"Aye, I shouldn't be surprised if we're for the gallows," the man said with a cold-sounding snigger in his voice. "If we're not to leave on our backs, though, we'll have to find a way out of here on our feet, but we'll not be staying, either way."

Thomas did not reply, but Alec had heard him say to others who contemplated escape that such attempts only brought trouble to all, and relief to none. The long history of successful escapes from the prison, though, kindled hope in the hearts of some of the company of prisoners, and was the subject of many late-night discussions between the bunks.

The apparent leader of the newcomers lifted one of the dimly-glowing braziers from the floor by its rickety handle. "Going to go have a look around the rest of the mine. Anything I ought beware of?"

"Only don't get lost back there," Thomas said. "It's a large loop, pierced through with a few passages, but if you stick to the right-hand wall, you should find your way back here in due course. Floor's rougher back there than here, but it's relatively level throughout, no large pits or holes."

"Thankee," the newcomer said curtly, and moved off into the darkness, his form visible only as a darker shadow against the dim red glow of the brazier.

The other two men settled down into their bunks, their deep breathing shortly giving way to alternating snores. It would have been funny, save that all knew they were going to have to try to find a way to sleep through the racket.

At the far end of the table, Alec could hear Thomas conferring quietly with some of the other men.

"They are going to bring trouble and punishment down on us all," one man hissed, loudly enough for Alec to hear him.

The others shushed him, and Alec could make out no more of the discussion, save for a low, grumbling murmur of men unsure what to expect of the next hours and days.

Most of the prisoners had drifted away from the table to their bunks, blankets pulled over to warm themselves in the perpetual chill of the chamber, when the newcomer's voice could be heard from the tunnels, hallooing and calling out to his companions.

"Leonard, James, raise your lazy bones! I've things to show you, things to discuss." The dim glow of the charcoal in the tin brazier could be seen approaching, far behind where his voice seemed to have been in the echoing, unpredictable acoustics of the tunnels.

Both of the other newcomers started groggily from their bunks at the sound of their names, and the stouter of the two grabbed his companion by the elbow, saying, "Charles has found something, from the sound of it. Come along, step lively."

After they had left, following the tunnel where the faint red glow of the charcoal illuminated the walls, the prisoners who had already gone to their bunks were left to grumble and roll themselves back into positions of relative comfort.

Alec figured there was little point in trying to get to sleep before the newcomers returned, as they clearly had no consideration for their fellows, so he remained at the table, quietly thinking over the letter his father had sent.

It sounded as though his father anticipated that the war would soon be over, and the British victorious, and was sure enough of it to urge Alec to make plans on that basis. Even if he was wrong, he made a cogent point in his contention that Alec's position was similar to that of other sons of Tories, save that this son was dozens of feet underground. Worse, Alec knew that he had no great hope of quickly emerging a free man, whether or not the British should win the war.

If the rebels were able, somehow, to strike a decisive blow, and bring the contest to an unhappy end, it was hard for Alec to envision his release coming with anything but the most crippling of restrictions. If the British should win, their priorities would be the exchange of their captive officers for American officers they held, then their own soldiers, and finally what Loyalist militias they cared to remember still existed.

Worse, he'd heard no news that convinced him the war would do anything but continue for the indefinite future. He was all too keenly aware that the rebel forces could retreat nearly endlessly, giving up nothing but Indian lands for as far as they went. The Crown gave every appearance of being able to go on sending fresh recruits and mercenaries, as well as continuing to appeal to the patriotic fervor of their colonial subjects, effectively without end. Both sides subsisted on foraging the communities through which they passed, taking what they needed by force or by fiat, with promissory notes only as good as the men who signed them.

Alec thought about the newcomers, then, and the harsh words of their leader. Was escape actually possible? He had to confess that he'd not given the matter much thought. The guards were armed and the prisoners were not, and that seemed the end of it. No man wanted to end his days gasping through a bayonet wound, or feeling his life's blood soak into the soil around him, so the slim chance of overmatching the guards through sheer force of numbers had never seemed one worth seriously contemplating.

There were few enough prisoners that even if the guards only shot or bayoneted a handful of their number, the chances were relatively high that it would be his grave dug next. Nobody was willing to roll those dice... but the newcomers sounded as though they believed they had nothing to lose.

If they actually were marked for death, then there was no reason to wait quietly for it to come escort them from the field. And even if they weren't under a death sentence, their demeanor suggested that they were accustomed to acting with recklessness toward the prospect.

If the newcomers did make a break for freedom, Alec wondered whether he might find an opportunity to join them, and so put himself into a position where he could, just possibly, consider the pursuit of Miss Landry's hand.

He realized with a jolt that the thought of such a pursuit was one that actually appealed to him now, so he supposed that his father had made his case persuasively enough on that front.

But had he any business putting his life – or what little remained of his father's legacy – at risk for a chance at that prospect? What good would it be to take a step in the direction of furthering the family name, only to have it come to rest in an early grave? There seemed no way out of the disagreement with his father, other than making the elder Tinsworth see that his only viable option was to wait and see what fortune might cast into his path.

To do that, he knew that he needed to be able to sit down and talk with his father, so the offered visit was a necessity. He resolved to ask Jonas in the morning to help him pen a letter in reply to his father, inviting him to return to the prison as soon as it was convenient.

He got up from the table, noticing that he was the last of the company still awake – other than the newcomers, down their tunnel someplace. Curling up on his bunk, he did his best to get comfortable and warm, knowing that both efforts were futile.

Alec knew that there could be no joy for his father in seeing his own son reduced to hard labor and imprisonment alongside the lowest ranks of society, and he appreciated how difficult it must be to endure each visit, so he appreciated his father's offer to return soon.

And, of course, there was always the possibility that

he might bring Miss Landry along with him, and that pleasant thought occupied his mind as he began to drift off to sleep. His nascent dreams were interrupted, though, by the return of the newcomers.

The men came into the sleeping chamber laughing and trading ribald jokes, and their leader said to the other two, "Sleep well, friends, and know that we begin tomorrow. We shall have our freedom before the summer."

Alec couldn't resist speaking into the darkness. "Do you mean to dig through the back tunnel? As you do so, have a care, as there's a pair of corpses somewhere in that rubble, men who thought they could dig their way to freedom a few years back."

A long silence answered him, and then an answer followed.

"Then we'll have to dig smarter and work twice as hard to preserve ourselves, shan't we?" A low chuckle sounded from the man's throat, sounding like menace embodied. "Thankee for the warning, whoever you may be."

Chapter 14

It was almost entertaining, watching the new prisoners being forced to undertake the same labors as the rest. A long day before the forge, under Gad's watchful eye, took the fight out of the lot of them, and at the end of the day, they were wearier than those who had become accustomed to the work before their arrival.

That and the moment spent dictating a brief reply to his father, inviting him to visit whenever he was able, and proposing that they should discuss the matter of Miss Landry in person, had been the only light moments in Alec's day.

He'd heard some of the other men discussing in low tones amongst themselves, when Gad and Jonas were distracted, whether to join in the newcomers' efforts at escape. Alec said nothing, but also did not join in on the discussions. Having heard nothing novel about their planning, he suspected that those who attempted escape would fail, and even if their consequences were not so dire as the men who supposedly still lay under the tons of rock that had fallen to stop their striving, Alec expected that he'd see these men on the post sooner or later.

Despite the history of escapes from the prison, that had all happened before the guards had brought it under modern management. Furthermore, the guards were as aware of the history as the prisoners, and so were on high alert for any new attempt.

All of this, of course, made the discussions, furtive though they may have been, even more fraught, and Alec caught himself wondering whether he ought to have a word with Jonas about the bold intentions of the three new prisoners. Then he remembered what had happened to the last man suspected of informing, and decided firmly to keep his concerns to himself. The guards wouldn't stripe everyone's backs over an escape attempt, would they?

After Alec finished dictating the letter to his father, though, he glanced around to be sure that no prisoners were in sight, and then asked quietly, "Are those new prisoners indeed bound for the gallows, as they told us?"

Jonas looked up sharply from the page he was folding, his startled expression giving way to a guffaw. "No, no, they're not to be hanged," he said, smiling wryly. "If they had been under a sentence of death, they never would have been sent here. No, they will stay in our custody with the rest of you, until you are paroled, exchanged, or ordered released for some other reason."

Alec gave him a questioning look.

Jonas looked thoughtful, and added, "Of course, parole is unlikely, but I've heard that the King's Navy holds a large number of prisoners on dismasted hulks in New-York Harbor, so 'tis possible that we'll exchange the lot of you for our own men at some point."

He shrugged. "And the last likely depends on the progress of the war, one way or t'other. I've not heard any intelligence that either encourages or discourages me on that question, so I'd not look for relief from that quarter, were I in your shoes."

Alec nodded slowly. "Our prospects for release are much as I'd thought. I am relieved, though, to understand that the new prisoners are not at risk of a noose."

Jonas grinned, his eyes twinkling almost malevolently. "Not yet, at least. 'Tis always possible for one of you fellows to commit some act so outrageous that we have no choice but to try and punish you for it. Not that I'm eager for that to happen, mind you, but neither will I shrink from it, should it become necessary." His smile faded as he spoke, and he shrugged brusquely. "In any event, you've tarried long enough up here; best that you join the others of your company."

"Aye, sir." Alec turned to go.

"Oh, and if those three raise any trouble down there, it would be best for everyone if someone gave us some warning of it, and did not leave us to discover it on our own. Silence is collaboration, and you can spread that word throughout the group."

Alec paused to hear Jonas out, nodded in acknowledgment, and went on to begin the descent into the darkness.

In the lodgings, there was little talk about the table, which was lit faintly with a single sputtering taper. Thomas pushed a torn hunk of bread into Alec's hands, along with a cold slice of greasy meat. He said quietly, "I know that you've been managing a correspondence with your father through Jonas, but mind that you don't tarry too often with him, lest some of the less restrained of our number come to believe that you're turning informant."

Alec answered just as quietly, "I'm no fool, and I marked well the story of the accident suffered by a man who was suspected of informing before my arrival... but thank you for the warning. I've done no informing whatever, but I have gathered some intelligence which you may be interested to hear."

Thomas cocked his eyebrow, the expression just visible in

the poor light, but said nothing.

Alec continued, his tone lowering even further. "They're no closer to the gallows than you or I, but are only putting on airs. I suspect it is to somehow better their position within our little society here."

Thomas nodded. "I don't doubt that you have the right of it. Still, they seem to be more interested than most new arrivals in finding a way to escape, and it might profit a careful man to see how they could be encouraged in this."

Alec gaped at the other man, but Jonas continued, unperturbed.

"Man's not meant to live in a box, and it's only the more ironic that they jail us in the name of defending their precious liberties. King George but asks them to pay a stamp tax, and they proceed to open revolt, yet they can justify putting us into a hole into the ground."

Thomas shook his head dismissively. "I shan't preach; I know you sing in this same choir. 'Tis but passing strange, and it begs the question of our obligations to remain in their bondage, that's all."

Alec nodded slowly, saying, "I suppose that I hadn't had time yet to consider it, but your words make sense."

"Aye. Regardless, rather than obstructing our new fellows, I think we'd do well to see how we might be able to assist them." He got a faraway look in his eye for a long moment, and then clapped Alec on the shoulder. "Indeed, I might have just the opportunity."

He raised his voice enough to be heard at the far end of the table, where the newcomers sat hunched together, their heads close, and their discussion in a confidential undertone. "You new boys might like to hear this, as it has bearing on your plans."

Charles rose, a frown etched into his face as though chiseled there at birth. His voice was gruff and suspicious. "Aye?"

"Aye," Thomas said. "Come on over here, so that I need not shout it loud enough for the guard to hear from above."

Charles made his way down to where Thomas and Alec sat, and slid himself onto the bench beside Alec.

Thomas said, "You're bound and determined to effect an escape from this place."

It wasn't a question, but Charles answered, "Better than waiting to rot or fall to disease in this wretched air." The big man waved a hand around through the charcoal-scented dimness.

"You'll get no argument from me, and indeed, I may have a means to advance your prospects."

"I'm listening," Charles said, and Thomas nodded, grinning.

"I thought you might. I'm expecting a package of necessaries from my sister within the fortnight. The last time I saw her, she and I agreed that if I ever asked after our aunt Ida, I meant that the time for action was drawing close. I've not yet done so, but I propose to do so when she comes."

"And what can a woman do to aid us in getting out of a hole half a hundred feet under the ground, through a bolted door of iron, past the guards, over the fence, and clear to freedom, all before an alarm can be raised?"

"That is where I think that the project you had proposed can help," Thomas said.

"Allow me to hazard a guess – you think that allowing one of us to be brained by a falling rock, or better yet, obliterated entirely, will provide a sufficient diversion to permit the rest of you to escape?"

"Nay, not at all. Indeed, we need to keep every one of our number healthy and hale in order for this to work."

Charles gave him a skeptical look.

"We'll have to leave behind any man who cannot lift himself up the rope that I'll have my sister put down the back shaft."

Charles' eyebrows rose, and Thomas hastened to explain.

"There were originally two shafts dug down to the level of the copper ore in this layer," he said. "The shorter one we use today to access our lodgings. The other one was blocked up after one of their first prisoners escaped, some years back, but I happen to know that the job of blocking it up was not so perfect as the guards would like to believe it was."

He paused, and Charles answered, "You've got my attention. I suppose you know how to direct your sister to find the opening of this back shaft?"

"Oh, aye," Thomas said. "It lies well outside the walls of this compound. Back in the day, they used to post a guard over it, but after they shut it up, they decided they no longer needed to do that."

"And what gives you reason to believe that it is not perfectly sealed up?" Charles' rough tone was becoming something closer to crafty, with a tinge of excitement. "If this is the case, that's certainly easier than trying to open up a new passage, particularly as we know that doing so has cost two men their lives already."

"Aye," Thomas said. "The shaft was only filled with what rock and soil they could easily lay their hands on, and it was in no way tamped down or settled. I am certain of this, because in cold weather, it admits a draft, and when there is rain in the world above, it drains right down through the old shaft without apparent resistance."

"How do you propose to remove the rock and soil undetected, and without greater risk than we are exposed to by digging anew?" The tone of Charles' voice had returned to skepticism, and his face looked hard and closed to Alec.

"The guards have not ventured down here to the tunnels in some time, and I do not suppose that they are likely to do so for any light reason. Even if they should come underground, they are not likely to inspect every corner of the catacombs. You've explored the chambers back there. Is there not plenty of space where we could put nearly any given amount of displaced fill?"

Charles nodded. "Aye, but how do we go about displacing it?"

Thomas leaned forward, speaking in a lower tone, so that Charles and Alec leaned forward instinctively, so as to be able to hear him.

"The second shaft is down the left-hand tunnel, nearly at the very end. You may have seen a passage off the far wall that ends in rubble? That's where the fill dropped into the tunnel from above."

With a motion of his hands, Thomas pantomimed scooping with his bare hands and said, "I propose to carry it away gradually, with but a few men working down there at any given time, and to take what we displace down into the last of the tunnels that communicate between the two sides of the mine. If we have to fill it up completely, I rather doubt that anyone would be the wiser – until it is too late, anyway."

His hands now described the fall of material from overhead, and he said, "As we draw away the rubble at the bottom, what is lodged above it in the shaft will naturally drop down, but only so suddenly as we remove its support from below, so I do not anticipate that the risk will be that great." He shrugged. "If things jam up, someone will have to work it loose, but I expect that we can arrange our work to keep those falls small and manageable."

Thomas sat back and awaited Charles' response.

The larger man sat with his mouth pursed, as though he'd drunk tea steeped too long. Finally, he nodded. "It could work. And once the shaft is clear, you simply ask your sister about the health of Aunt Ida, and we make for the surface with the guards none the wiser until we fail to answer their call in the morning."

"That's the idea, yes," Thomas answered.

Charles' expression was still not that of one who is wholly convinced, but he continued to nod slowly to himself. "It sounds like the work of months, and getting the men to agree to such hard work after their labors in making nails – nails, for all love! – may prove difficult."

"Aye," said Thomas, "though the prospect of freedom is likely to help them forget their weariness. I worry, though, about being detected by the amount of grime we will accumulate about our persons, above what we already naturally carry. A man who swings a hammer or pumps bellows may become filthy, but he is unlikely to get that filth under his fingernails or into his hair. The guards may well take note if we cannot conceal the fact that we are working on two different jobs, for different masters."

Charles nodded more vigorously now. "We could tell the guards that we are enlarging our living quarters down here, though, as we've gotten too cramped together, and tell them that we ask for nothing but their leave to do so?"

Thomas thought about the idea for a moment.

Alec wasn't sure that the guards would have any sympathy for their charges being too close, or underfed, or poorly clothed. After all, if the rebel troops in the field suffered privation, tending to the needs of prisoners could be seen as taking food right out of the mouths of their own men in favor of their enemies. On the other hand, letting prisoners see to their own needs, so long as it cost the rebels nothing, might appeal.

Thomas said slowly, "Jonas would probably go along, but Gad will tell us that we aren't meant to be living in luxury, and if we wanted more space, we ought to switch sides and fight for the American cause." He spat, underscoring his distaste for that idea.

Alec ventured to speak up for the first time. "I think that while Gad may oppose it, Jonas is likely to tell him to stay out of our way. The rest of the guard will follow their lead, of course. Just to be safe, we probably ought actually do some visible work to enlarge this chamber, so that if they come down to check on us, they may be satisfied as to our trustworthiness."

Charles laughed, a bark of sound that chopped off as quickly as it erupted. "This one's a clever lad. You ought keep a close eye on him, friend."

Thomas smiled quickly, and answered, "Aye, and he's not wrong. The ruse must be as complete as possible, lest the guards find reason to be suspicious."

Charles said, "Very well, let us try to enact this plan; if the guards tell us we may not work to better ourselves, then we can try other ways to address the problem of removing ourselves from the grasps of these traitors to our sovereign."

He nodded briskly in dismissal, and stood up to return to the other end of the chamber where his friends waited.

Chapter 15

Alec watched from his station at the forge, waiting for the bellows to drive the first heat of the morning as Thomas spoke with Jonas, his head held low, deferential. Jonas looked up at Thomas, his expression at first skeptical, and then suspicious. He asked Thomas something, and the prisoner answered quietly.

Jonas gestured toward the guardhouse, shaking his head. Thomas appeared to answer him, his hands rising in a pleading motion, but Jonas shook his head again and directed Thomas back to his own workstation by the forge.

Thomas caught Alec's eye and shook his head minutely. There would be no cover story for men's hands getting dirtied and bruised by labor under the earth.

Alec sighed and checked the heat on the forge. He didn't know what form Charles' response would take, but he was certain that the brusque, ruthless man would not hesitate to take matters into his own hands.

Just before midday, the work at the forges was disrupted by a visitor, welcomed through the main gate by Jonas. Alec's father entered the walled compound, and Alec was overcome with joy to see the man again so soon.

Ignoring Gad's scowl, Alec nodded at Jonas with a grin as the guard waved him to the gate to greet his father.

This time opting for a more dignified handshake, Alec said, "Thank you for coming so quickly upon receiving my letter, sir."

"I could do no other thing," his father said, drawing Alec into an embrace.

So much for remaining dignified.

When his father stood back, holding Alec by the shoulders and examining him, Alec said, uncomfortably, "I am not much changed since last you saw me."

"That may be," his father replied, "but I should like to reassure myself of that. The labor of working at the forge is broadening your shoulders from those of a boy into your proper adult stature. There is something new in the way you regard the world, too, that I've not seen before."

He released his son, and the two of them walked toward the guardhouse together, mindful of the glances of guards and prisoners alike. Alec's father said, "I hope that my presence here does not cause you difficulty once I depart."

"Nay, it gives them something to speculate upon, and me something to think on, without fail."

His father nodded. "Well, let me give you something to think on, then, since you said that you wished to discuss the matter of Miss Landry in person."

"Aye, I did."

It occurred to Alec, though he did not give voice to his thought, that he had hoped thereby to forestall any such discussion until a time when it would be but academic, with Miss Landry safely married off to a more likely suitor.

"I have spoken with Miss Landry's father, and he has acquainted me with certain facts that I feel obligated to pass along to you, that you may include them in your considerations."

Alec's eyebrow went up, but he said nothing, and his father continued.

"First, there is the question of Miss Landry herself. If I may speak bluntly, I am aware that she is probably rather plain in comparison with some of the girls you've chanced to meet in your travels."

Alec opened his mouth to object, but his father raised a hand to silence him, and said with a grim smile, "Her father noted that you avoided looking at her while she attended to your haircut and shaving. I want you to understand that a comely face rarely stays that way over the years of a partnership, and a finely-formed ankle grows thick and well-used in the course of a worthy life."

He sighed. "Basing a decision for all of your life on the appearance of youth is the worst kind of short-sighted thinking. I urge you to look beyond it, if you cannot find the charms of Miss Landry's form, or that of any other girl you may consider in her stead, for that matter."

Alec wanted to protest, but his father's words had struck home, at least so far as his observation that he'd not let his gaze rest on Miss Landry's face; however, it had been out of respect for her and not wishing to appear to be staring with too much familiarity.

Before he could explain himself, his father was continuing on.

"Further, it is my experience that it is exceptionally rare that one could not find some element of beauty in any woman's face, if only one is inclined to look for it, without spending too much time focusing on what faults may lie there. Contrariwise, even the most perfect face will inevitably carry some flaw, if one looks hard enough for it. 'Tis but a matter of your motivation, what you seek after as you look."

He raised two fingers now and said, "Second, there is the question of whether Miss Landry would even consider you a suitable partner. While it would be indelicate of me to inquire directly, and equally indelicate for her father – or Miss Landry herself – to state the matter plainly, I believe that should you approach her with the question of whether you may court her, you would find a favorable reception."

He appeared to be about to add something else, but he stopped himself, and held up another finger, his thumb holding his index finger down firmly. "Third, there is the matter of Miss Landry's prospects, and your own. While you are, at present, in the custody of our restive American cousins, we both know that this condition cannot last forever, but will come to an end one way or another."

Alec looked around to see whether any of the guards were in earshot, and said, "Aye, one way or another," but left it at that as his father nodded in absent agreement.

Alec was still pondering the incredible thought that Miss Landry was apparently receptive to his potential pursuit of her hand, so he almost missed what his father said next.

"Mister Landry gave me to understand that Miss Landry has a childless uncle back in England, and that this uncle has designated her as his heir, by way of providing a dowry on hearing the news of Mister Landry's dispossession of his American holdings."

Seeing Alec's look of confusion, he chuckled. "Your Miss Landry stands to become not a wealthy woman, but a comfortable one, with sufficient income from her future land holdings to support her husband's pursuit of a life of meaningful matters, far better than manual labor of any sort."

"Of course, this would necessitate that she and her husband assume residence on the estate in England, but whichever way this contest ends, I do not see these shores being all that welcoming to those of us who opposed the American cause. They will either resent us for our success, or take their vengeance upon us in their victory. In either case, none of us has much here still to hold us, as I have said to you in the past."

He placed his hand on Alec's shoulder, and said, "Whatever you may decide regarding Miss Landry, you ought not plan on remaining in America at the end of this accursed war. I have been making careful inquiries among my family and friends in England, and I have reason for confidence that I will be able to secure a place for us."

Alec nodded. "I had already reached much the same conclusion," he said. "I will give the question of Miss Landry more careful consideration, informed by these facts." He took a deep breath, and added, "Indeed, I half-expected you to bring her along to bolster your case for my consideration of her finer qualities."

His father laughed heartily. "I must confess that the idea crossed my mind, but I did not wish to appear to be pressing you too dearly in the matter. Nor could I have spoken so plainly in her presence."

Suddenly wishing to clear the air of the primary question that had plagued him ever since the possibility of a match with Miss Landry had been raised, Alec asked, "Has Miss Landry no other possible suitors, out of all of the young men of the district? Has she truly fallen so far in our society that a man who rots underground in a rebel prison is her best available choice?"

His father smiled sadly at Alec. "You are not so low as that among your friends, son. You've accepted a man's responsibilities in your service in defense of our sovereign's interests, and your captivity is but a mark of that service. When your name is discussed, it is with respect and sympathy. You are not classed with the common criminals who are the natural residents of a place such as this, never fear that for a moment."

Alec nodded slowly, wanting to believe, and his father went on.

"When your time within these walls has been ended, you will find yourself accorded a hero's welcome in our community. You may rely on that without fail."

Alec persisted, asking, "And of others who might make suit for Miss Landry's hand? What of them?"

His father dismissed the thought with a wave of his hand. "Fled like field mice before a hawk, or else taken in battle, by death or to imprisonment like yours. Oh, there might be one or two soft, frightened boys still about the district, but Miss Landry would no more consider them than she would consider one of your common criminals in this place. No, you are her most appealing option, both for your own charms as she may see them, and as an objective matter."

Alec couldn't help but feel a surge of pride in himself, for the first time since that miserable night in the woods when he had fallen for an elementary ruse of the rebels who'd brought him here. It had been hard to think of himself as anything but a base failure since then, but his father's words gave him the first reassurance that his sacrifice was seen as worthwhile.

He wondered what the community of Loyalists would think of him if he were to escape. Would he be hailed as a hero then, or seen as having dishonorably evaded this portion of his service to King and country? Or was it his duty to King and country to undertake every possible effort to resist his captors and escape from them as quickly as he could?

His mind roiled with questions that he knew were too risky to give voice to in proximity to the guards of this prison, but he couldn't stop pondering them within the safe confines of his own mind. If he were to escape, would he be obliged to return to his service in the militia, or would his duty be considered as having been discharged completely? Would the rebels pursue him all the way to the door of his home, or would they view escaped Loyalist militiamen no more than a nuisance?

His father was looking at him with a bemused expression, and said, "Ha'pence for your thoughts, son."

Alec shook his head. "Naught that I can speak aloud, Father." He came to a sudden decision. "Please bid Miss Landry to visit us again here and attend to our barbering soon, if the guards will permit it."

His father gave him a smile of understanding, and returned it with interest. "Aye, I will see if I can make the arrangements before I go." He added hopefully, "Is there aught I can tell her in addition?"

Alec shook his head, smiling gently. "I think that I should see whether I can discover for myself the many fine qualities that you have mentioned, and then make my decision with the benefit of her counsel."

His father smiled broadly. "You are off to a good start,

then. I shall take my leave and let you return to your labors here."

He stood and drew Alec into another tight embrace, which seemed to be their new normal greeting and farewell, strange as it seemed to Alec.

"I hope to see you again soon, son. Be well."

As Alec watched the man walk away in the company of the guard, he said to his receding back, "Be well, father."

Chapter 16

Dinner that night was some sort of porridge made with peas and maybe a scrap of greasy meat somewhere in it, but the food wasn't what had Alec's stomach in knots. Charles and Thomas were engaged in a heated discussion, albeit at low enough volume that they could not be heard at the top of the mine shaft – or so Alec hoped, at least.

Charles hadn't taken well the news of Jonas' refusal to do any sort of tunneling work whatsoever. After discussing with Thomas the reasons that Jonas gave – primarily, he did not want the prisoners to wear themselves out and render themselves unfit for the labor they were assigned – Charles moved on to arguing with Thomas over the question of the proposed enlargement of their living quarters. He seemed almost to have forgotten that the work was a ruse intended to cover their actual project.

"Does he expect us to do nothing to better ourselves, permit us no latitude to improve our condition?"

"Aye, 'tis exactly his purpose. In the end, he cares not whether we are comfortable or even particularly safe. His charge is to keep us in confinement until such time as he is told that he need no longer do so. If we survive that time, that is to his credit; if he can extract from us some labor, it improves his own situation further, without reference to whether it benefits us."

Charles said nothing for a long moment, but his already

substantial bulk seemed to swell even further. Finally, he practically exploded, hissing, "And you mean to just accept that?"

Thomas answered quietly, "Nay, but I am satisfied to let Jonas think that I have."

Charles favored him with a sour look, and then asked, "What exactly do you mean by that?"

Thomas looked at the larger man steadily and said, "I mean that we ought proceed on the original plan, and take our chances that our efforts will leave some visible mark on those who undertake it."

Charles snorted. "So, what you're saying is that you've no helpful addition to make to the original plan of digging our way out of here, save that we ought dig into a vertical shaft, one which will require the assistance of your sister to escape through, instead of clearing a tunnel to the surface through which we may depart unaided?"

Thomas said, "Aye, though 'tis not so simple nor as nefarious as that. It is my honest assessment that the old shaft offers the greatest chance of success, with the lowest risk of harm. This mine has claimed too many already, a portion of both prisoners and those who were but attempting to make an honest living here."

Charles' mouth pursed as he considered Thomas' case. Finally, he nodded. "Very well. We ought begin at once, then, as the sooner we are out of the control of these rebel fiends, the better off we will be."

Thomas nodded, though Alec thought that his expression was far from demonstrating agreement with Charles, and then he made his way to where the rest of the prisoners had gathered, trying to stay out of the obvious power struggle.

Thomas took a deep breath before committing himself. Alec could see that the leader knew that he was taking a great risk in sharing the plan with all of the prisoners, as any one of them might be an informer.

"Gentlemen, we have agreed upon a plan for our mutual escape. It has become apparent that our jailers intend to work us to death, making nails that they sell for their own benefit, while claiming that the income is used only for our maintenance."

He gestured at the empty bowl that had contained the poor meal they'd just finished.

"The food we receive is not noticeably improved over what we were fed when we did not labor, and we have had no new clothes or blankets, nor any other item of comfort since the start of our industry."

A general murmur of agreement rose from the lot, and Alec could only admire Thomas' skill at bringing men of a wide array of backgrounds and temperaments into agreement all at once. Thomas wasn't done, though.

"As most of us are held here as prisoners for the duration of the war, we may have hoped for relief at the end of the contest, yet what intelligence we can glean from beyond the walls of our jail gives little hope that the war will come to an end within the foreseeable future.

"Therefore, our best hope of leaving this place alive is by escape, and we have worked out a plan for that. It will require greater labors than ever, and it is not without risks, but I will remind you that this prison, for all that it is a miserable place to be held, has permitted a remarkable record of escapes in the past."

A chuckle went around the room, and one prisoner said,

"Aye, and a remarkable record of prisoners dying in the attempt, too. Let's hear your plan, and how you hope to avoid adding to that tally, eh?"

Thomas nodded and said, "A very good point. All of the available avenues for escape come along with some chance of harm coming to us, whether at the hands of our jailers, or from the chances of nature. We've given consideration to all of these in devising our present plan, but if you've something to say once I tell you what we propose, then say it."

"Oh, I shall," the man replied, but raised no further objections, and Thomas nodded.

"When this was a working copper mine, there was a second shaft sunk to this level for the purpose of removing ore. That shaft lies outside the boundaries of the prison walls overhead, and though it has been filled in, I believe it was done haphazardly, and that we can readily enough open it, and so effect our escape without detection."

"Is it back by where the draft flows on windy days?"

The question came from one of the men who'd been in the jail with Thomas nearly since it had been re-opened.

"Aye, that's the place."

The man nodded. "The matter below there looks as though it would remove easily enough, with the application of proper tools or enough brute strength."

"Strength we have, though we're denied tools, for self-evident reasons."

Another chuckle went around the group.

"When are we to work at this feat, then?"

"After we complete our daily labors in the nail

manufacture."

Thomas raised a hand to forestall the grumbling and moans from several of the men. "I know that it is asking a great deal of you, but the possibility of regaining our freedom is worth any measure, is it not? Our rebellious friends like to shout from the rooftops about the sacrifices they make for freedom, but here we have a real opportunity to show them what steps common men are willing to take to win freedom from their homegrown tyranny."

Thomas looked around the group, their faces faintly illuminated in the greasy light of the single candle. "Who's with us, then?"

Charles raised his hand immediately. "I am."

His friends looked slightly startled, and then both of them raised their hands, as well. Other hands came up, some tentative, others more assured, and in the end, only a few men sat with their arms crossed or down in their pockets.

Glancing from one face to the next, Thomas nodded gravely. "We begin at once. Let those who do not wish to join us stay back to raise the alarm, should our guards choose this moment to pay us a visit. Are you willing to do that much?"

One of the men with his arms still crossed over his chest nodded, his face set in a grimace. "I'm willing to stand guard against our guards, aye, but I think that your effort is likely to come to naught. We've no way to climb a shaft, even if we can clear it."

Thomas grinned. "Aye, I forgot to tell you of that part, didn't I? My sister will drop a rope down the shaft once we've got it opened, and we'll be able to depart at our convenience, dispersing into the country around, such that none of our company shall ever be found."

The man's skeptical look gave way to a thoughtful expression, but he said, "Still don't think there's any way to clear that shaft, but if you can make that happen, I can stay here and keep watch easily enough." He looked around at the other three men who'd kept their hands down.

Two were among the criminal prisoners, and the third was a scared-looking private from the Tory militias. The militiaman said nothing, but bit his lip, as though trying to stop himself from crying out in terror at the thought of being caught trying to escape, while the two criminals both stood and went to their bunks without a word, either to one another, or to the self-appointed ringleader of the refusers.

The main objector said to Thomas curtly, "I don't expect you'll get any trouble from our lot. Go and make your effort."

Thomas bowed slightly and picked up the candle, motioning to the others to follow him into the mine's tunnels.

Chapter 17

Alec collapsed into his bunk and pulled the blanket up over himself. He had no idea of the hour, but the past eternity had been an endless succession of rocks, passed hand-to-hand from one man to the next, moving them from the pile at the base of the old shaft to the tunnel where Thomas had decided to put the debris.

His back ached, his hands were bruised from those rocks which had been passed over less gently than was ideal, and he felt certain that his arms would fall out of their sockets entirely if he had to work as long for a second night in a row.

However, after Thomas had called a halt for the night, the prisoners had filed past the open face of the dig on their way back to the sleeping quarters, and Alec had been gratified to see that they had already made visible progress at clearing the initial pile. Already, the worked side of the opening into the shaft above was exposed at the front of the pile, and Alec could see that the rocks wedged up in the shaft would start to tumble free with the removal of just another few feet of material from under them.

At that thought, he was thankful that he had been placed toward the middle of the group, as he had an unreasoning fear of being crushed beneath rocks falling from overhead, a fear driven by nightmares that had awoken him more than once since he had come to this place.

He was still thinking about how the men working the face of the dig might avoid being struck, when he drifted into sleep. It seemed to him that there had been no passage of time whatsoever when he heard the clanging of the pots at the entrance to the mine.

"Time to move, you lazy sods," Gad called down. "There's work to be done, and the sun's already up, with nobody manning the forges. Come get your meal and start earning your daily bread, you bunch of lousy traitors and thieves."

Alec could hear the thud of the basket that contained their morning meal as it hit the bottom of the shaft, and he groaned as he hauled himself out of his bunk. Doubtless, whatever food had been sent down would now be spilled in the dirt and covered with grit and filth.

He would not miss Gad when he was free of this place.

After the prisoners had broken their fast – stale loaves of bread with added dirt to grind between their teeth, and a cheese that had, thankfully, been wrapped in cloth – they headed aboveground for their day's labors. Everyone seemed short-tempered, including the guards, and by the time the forges were hot, there had already been words exchanged on a couple of occasions.

The weather seemed to have also been affected by the mood of the men, with heavy, grey clouds spitting cold rain down on the compound. The man carrying iron stock over to Alec's forge slipped in the mud and dropped the iron in a confused tangle at his feet, although by good fortune, nobody was hurt. Other minor accidents followed all day, and when Jonas finally whistled to signal the end of the shift, Alec breathed a sigh of relief that there hadn't been any serious mishaps.

As the men streamed into the guardhouse and began descending into the mine, Jonas motioned Alec aside.

"Son, I noticed that you lot seemed out of sorts today. Is there aught I should know about, some conflict that has disrupted the group?"

His heart suddenly hammering in his throat, Alec said, "Nay, sir, 'tis only that one of the new men snores so loudly that it has been disrupting the sleep of everyone else in our company."

Jonas nodded, relief apparent in his expression. "Well, there's nothing to be done for that, but it does explain the request that Thomas made of me yesterday."

Alec faked a look of confusion, and Jonas explained, "He was asking whether the sleeping chamber could be expanded, to provide more space for the prisoners housed here."

Alec nodded, and then said, "May I go now? I fear that they will not save my ration for me, should I be delayed."

Jonas waved him toward the kitchen. "Certainly, go. You may tell them that I was inquiring as to whether you needed to send another letter to your father."

"Aye, sir, and I shall need to soon enough, if he hasn't already spoken with you."

"He has, so there is no need for further correspondence, unless you should feel the urge to discuss matters with him before his next visit." Jonas looked Alec in the eye, and Alec felt for a moment as though the guard were actually taking an interest in where matters stood between him and Miss Landry.

He dismissed the thought, and said only, "Nay, we came to a sufficient understanding at his last visit. Miss Landry will likely come and offer her barbering services to the company again."

Jonas nodded. "That would be most welcome, on the same terms as before. You may tell the men to expect her return, and I will make the necessary arrangements with your father."

"Aye sir, and thank you, sir." Alec turned to leave.

Behind him, Jonas said, more to himself than to Alec, "I imagine that everyone involved benefits from the arrangement in the end."

Alec smiled to himself as he swung down the ladder and into the mine.

Belowground, dinner was proceeding slowly and quietly. Thomas and Charles were conferring, and as Alec emerged from the mine shaft, Thomas raised a questioning eyebrow at him.

Alec explained, "Jonas wanted to ask after the arrangements to have Miss Landry return and barber the men. I told him to communicate with my father on the question."

He knew that his safety depended on being able to make the lie believable, even though he'd revealed nothing to the guard. It hardly seemed right that he should be suspected of turning traitor at both ends of the mine shaft, without having done anything amiss at either.

Thomas nodded, though, and returned to his discussion with Charles.

Alec sat down and spooned out his portion of dinner. Tonight, it was a broth thickened with ground corn, and while it wasn't particularly appetizing, it was filling, and the warmth of it helped dispel the underground chill.

After a time, Thomas stood up and spoke to the group. "We'll take a rest tonight, and only work for the duration of half the candle we have remaining. Tomorrow night, we'll try working without light, as we don't have any additional candles to spend on the effort."

Alec didn't much like the sound of that, particularly for the men working the face of the opening, where it might be important to be able to avoid falling rocks and debris. However, he knew that Charles and Thomas had both insisted on taking that duty, as they didn't want to ask anyone else to expose themselves to risks that they were not willing to take on themselves.

He hurried to finish eating, as most everyone else had already slurped down their shares, and they were starting to rise and head toward the tunnel.

The work that night seemed easier, in part because Alec knew that it would not go on for so long, and in part because there was a familiar rhythm to it now. Reach ahead in the tunnel, feel for the rock being passed to him, grasp it in his hands, and twist to deliver it to the man behind him. Over and over again, the movement repeated until it was almost more comfortable to keep moving than to contemplate holding still.

At the end of the time allotted, though, Alec was glad enough to return to his bunk, where he again fell into a deep sleep, and all night he dreamed that he was still rotating back and forth, moving stones from the face of the cut toward the side tunnel, passing them from hand to hand as part of one long, continuous machine made of men's hands and spines.

Chapter 18

The company of prisoners was perhaps two hours into their work the following night when disaster struck. Alec's first hint that something had gone awry was that the man in front of him left him twisted awkwardly, awaiting a rock that never came. At the same moment, Alec heard voices shouting from around the corner, where the face of the dig was, sounding calls for light.

Someone rushed past him in the darkness from the front of the line, hands out to both sides to find the walls, heedless of the men's chests, faces, and shoulders encountered along the way. After the man passed, Alec could guess at his progress by the grunts of surprise or objections rippling along the passageway, almost like another stone passing along the line.

Soon enough, the man returned, and Alec was unsurprised to see that it was Thomas, his face set in a grim expression – and the hand carrying the raised taper splattered with something dark and viscous. A few minutes after he'd passed, Thomas returned, stopping at the place where the line of men turned the corner, so that he could be heard and seen by all.

"We're done here for the night, and perhaps altogether. Return to your bunks and make as though you have been sleeping for hours. I must go and raise the guard, as there has been a death, and none of us want to sleep with a corpse among us, no matter how many questions it may raise to have it reported now."

A murmur among the men rose almost immediately to shouted questions.

"Who's died?"

"What happened?"

"What's to become of the project?"

"Who'd we lose?"

Thomas put his fingers to his lips and whistled for silence. "I'll answer what I can," he said. "The man who died was James, one of the number most recently added to our company. The dark concealed a wedged rock overhead, and when it came loose, it caught him at the crown of his head and struck him down instantly."

Thomas closed his eyes, as though willing the sight of the dead man's crushed head erased from his memory, then forced himself to continue. "I know not whether we will be able to conceal the cause of his death, but we will try to make a believable story that he was struck down by a rock falling onto his bunk."

Someone muttered, "That's easy enough to believe, as often as material falls from the ceilings."

Thomas answered, "Aye, 'tis at least a believable lie; the question will be whether or not our jailers can be persuaded to accept it as truth. We'll do best to make the story believable if we can appear to have been roused from a sound sleep by the disturbance, so let us return to our bunks and make them look as though they've seen use."

Thomas pointed back in the direction of their living quarters, and as the men turned to go, he caught Alec's eye. "You, come with me. We need help carrying James back to a bunk, along with the rock that ended him."

Alec gulped hard, but came along, following the flickering light of the taper back to the dig face.

There, he could see at once that three days of moving rocks had actually made a pretty substantial dent in the pile of rubble, and under a fresh spill of rock, James lay face-down, his fingers splayed out in a final grasping spasm at the uneven layer of rubble beneath him. Ironically, the smell of copper lay heavy in the air, but Alec recognized it as being the scent of blood.

Charles and Leonard sat forlornly by the corpse, and as soon as there was light, Charles rose and began mechanically removing rubble from atop James' back and shoulders. The rock atop the man's ruined skull was only a bit bigger than his head, but it appeared to be solid granite.

Thomas set down the crude candleholder, balancing it so that it would cast light over the lurid scene. He squatted beside the rock, wrapped his hands around it, and lifted it clear, grunting with the effort.

Alec heard him mutter, "Couldn't have managed to get himself flattened under anything lighter, I suppose," and Alec frowned, thinking it disrespectful of the dead in the presence of his friends, but the other two men gave no sign of hearing Thomas.

Alec approached and held out his hands to take the rock.

Thomas' eyebrows rose. "You think that a few weeks at the forge has given you that much strength? You're welcome to attempt it, of course, but I thought I would carry this back, while you and the other two took James."

Alec gave Thomas a grim look and motioned with his fingers for the other man to hand over the rock. Although he wasn't eager to take the blood-smeared granite, he was even less eager to handle yet another slack-limbed corpse.

Thomas shrugged and transferred the rock from his hands to Alec's.

It was heavier than Alec had anticipated, but he felt pretty certain that he'd be able to carry it all the way back.

Thomas motioned with his chin. "Get going, if you can make your way without light." He looked at the corpse again and added, "For that matter, we shall all need to make our way without light, unless that fellow can be persuaded to carry the candle. Alas, he is past reason or ability now, leaving the lot of us to carry everything in his stead."

He again jerked his head down the dark tunnel. "Go, and don't bother standing around, waiting for me to stop my meandering."

Alec nodded quickly and started down the way into darkness. Fortunately, the path was worn relatively smooth by the passage of many feet over the past few nights, so there were few obstacles on the ground.

The rock in his hands was heavy and slick, and he didn't care to think about what it was that was making it more difficult to maintain a hold on. He didn't mourn the dead man – he had scarcely gotten a chance to get to know him, other than as a menacing presence at Charles' side – but death was not a thing that Alec had become comfortable with.

He remembered the first time he'd seen somebody killed, a fellow militiaman struck down by a ball fired by some rebel hiding in a fencerow. One moment, they'd been marching along – if the uncoordinated shuffle of weary men moving yet again from one place to another could fairly be called a 'march' – and the next moment, the man was stumbling and falling almost before the report of the shot could reach Alec's ears.

He'd been among those who'd hurried to the stricken man's aid, and he had held the militiaman's cooling hand as his life's blood poured out through the ragged hole in his side. Someone had told him that there was no point in holding the man's hand, that he'd likely been dead before he hit the ground. Alec thought, though, that if he were ever the one to lay dying, he'd want his last awareness to be that someone cared enough to grant him one last sensation of human contact.

While a few men ranged out to try to find the killer, Alec had been rounded up with some of the other men to dig a grave.

As he walked in the darkness now, he grunted to himself at the memory, thinking that it seemed to be his lot in life to dig graves for others. He hadn't even known that first dead man's name, but the feeling of his slack fingers held in Alec's hand would haunt him to the end of his days.

He reached the living quarters, where he found that Thomas had profligately left a second taper lit, and lugged the rock over to where James had been sleeping, which was fortuitously a top bunk. He lifted the small boulder up to the height of his shoulder and slid it onto the rough planking of the bunk, sighing with relief at not having to carry it any further.

He turned and found that many of the prisoners were staring at him, including Daniel, whose wide-eyed gaze looked both awed and frightened by Alec's appearance.

He shook his head at them and walked over to his own bunk, wearily sitting down and gathering his blanket around himself. A noise from the tunnel made him look up, where he saw the strange sight of the dead man indeed holding the candle, his hands folded over the base of the candleholder to steady it on his own chest while the other three men carried him.

At Thomas' instructions, the trio brought him over to the bunk, and then hoisted the limp corpse up beside the rock Alec had placed there, the candleholder wobbling precariously, but not falling. Thomas retrieved the candle, and then moved the rock to rest beside the dead man's head, which he turned to foster the illusion that the granite stone had struck him down where he lay.

Thomas called Charles over, and together, they rolled James over to lie on his stomach, since the rock had struck him in the back of the head. He reached past the body to retrieve the man's blanket, and pulled it up over the corpse's shoulders, and Charles sat dazedly on his own bunk, beneath James'.

Standing back, Thomas examined the scene and shook his head. "Won't withstand even the most haphazard examination, but it will have to do," he grumbled to himself, and then squared his shoulders, turning toward the other men in their bunks. "All right, I'm going to go raise the alarm, as though we just heard the rock fall and were awakened by it."

A voice came from the darkness. "Just as though you were awakened by a rockfall, eh?"

Gad stepped into the light, and Alec felt as shocked and horrified into stillness as Thomas looked.

The guard stalked forward and growled, "Pity that the sound of your voices carries so well up the passages of this old mine, even if I could not make out what you were saying to one another." He turned to address Thomas. "And if you weren't awakened by a rockfall, what were you doing awake already at this advanced hour of the night, pray tell, sir?"

His nose wrinkled as the smell of blood reached him, and he whirled toward the bunks, his eyes roving over the prisoners, who seemed barely to dare to breathe – and one who did not breathe at all.

Striding toward James' bunk, he whipped off the blanket, puzzled, until his eyes reached the man's head.

"Have you again conspired together to commit murder, then? If so, you've chosen poorly this time – this man is no more an informer than any of you miserable worms." His glance fell to the floor, where Alec saw that a drop of blood glinted on the rocks.

Seizing up one of the tapers, Gad knelt and examined the spattered drop, and then spotted another, leading him toward the tunnel, and another, and the next.

His eyes narrowed, and he whirled, pulling back the front of his coat to exhibit the pistol he wore there. "Nobody move, or I'll shoot you down on the spot. I shall return in a trice, once I've discovered where the foul deed was committed."

Alec and the rest of the men watched, none moving any more than the rock over their heads did. He could feel his heart racing in his chest, seeming almost to strangle him as it leapt up toward his throat. In the span of no more than a score of shallow breaths, the light shone back down the tunnel as Gad returned, his face twisted into a victorious rictus of anger.

He spoke slowly, his tone low and deadly. "You dared dream of attempting to escape? You, who we have sworn to hold and protect here until our duties are discharged, were so bold as to start digging your way out of this space we've prepared for you? And I suppose that when one of your number risked an objection, you struck him down, thinking that you could make it look as though he had suffered an accident?"

Nobody answered him, and Gad shook his head grimly. "I have been telling Jonas that it would embolden you too much to take up some industry, and permit you to put on airs of being civilized men, but I never thought that I would be so swiftly and completely vindicated."

He started back toward the ladder, seizing the second candle from the table and extinguishing it with a vicious puff blown from a mouth that remained twisted in an expression that mingled joy and rage. Deliberately turning it sideways to let the melted tallow drip to the ground, he put the snuffed taper into his pocket, and lifted the other one to light his way, glancing around the frozen prisoners with disdain.

"I shall go now and report what you have done to Jonas, and if necessary, to the Committee of Safety and the Council itself, to ensure that justice will be done here. We shall doubtless return to determine which of you fiends should hang for this murder, and to take what measures we deem advisable to prevent you from making any further attempts at escape."

He sniffed. "I shouldn't imagine that you'll be permitted to come up into the yard any longer for the relief of wholesome work to do, oh, no. Enjoy your confinement and rest." His smile was filled with malice, and it was the last thing Alec saw before Gad whirled and left the living quarters for the entrance shaft, plunging the chamber into darkness.

Chapter 19

Although it seemed impossible, between the threat that stalked them from above the ground, and the corpse that kept them company below, Alec fell into a fitful sleep, punctuated by recurring nightmares where the nameless militiaman felled on the long-ago march turned his head to reveal that he had been struck down, not by a ball between his ribs, but by a granite boulder dropped by some unseen hand.

Others stirred restlessly around him, including Thomas, who still seemed stunned into permanent silence by the events of the night. For his part, Charles had been uncharacteristically silent and withdrawn, no murmur of conversation audible from his bunk. A couple of times, Alec thought he'd heard Leonard say something to him, but there had been no answer. Of course, Alec reflected, sleeping under the bunk holding the corpse of a dead friend was hardly a comforting position to be in.

On the other hand, it was possible that Charles had found some other empty bunk to move to in the darkness. There had been a few nearby, and Alec imagined that he would prefer to feel his way to some other place to seek rest, under the circumstances.

However, for the most part, Alec's conscious thoughts were not of the dead man or his brutish companions, but rather of his father. He felt quite certain that the easy arrangement of visits was at an end, and the thought gave him a keen sense of loss, that he had been looking forward to the potential to discuss with the elder Tinsworth the events of this disastrous night.

He found himself awake without even being aware of the transition from sleep to wakefulness, and laid in his bunk, his fingers moving slowly over its rough timbers, tracing out the grain of the wood in silent contemplation. He wondered what news would reach his father's ears, whether there would be any explanation, or just a flat refusal of further communication.

And what of Miss Landry? How could he even contemplate the possibility of pursuing her, if he could not so much as speak with her? The thought, he was surprised to realize, filled him with a sense of melancholy that bordered on outright despair.

His thoughts were interrupted by a loud clanging from the entrance shaft to the mine. Gad's voice called down, and Alec wondered whether the man ever slept, even before he grasped what the guard was saying.

"You'll find your rations at the bottom of the shaft. I'll be down with others shortly to retrieve your victim's body, and inform you of certain consequences of your night's activities — and to warn you of future events that you may anticipate."

The iron door clanged shut with such finality that it made Alec wonder whether Gad intended ever to open it again. He heard men shuffling about in the darkness, and while he knew that his eyes were as well adapted as they could possibly be to see in any light that might be offered to them, there was no light by which to see anything at all.

He sat up slowly and then stood to walk over to the tables. He barked his shin on a bench and gave a grumbled curse, but felt his way into a seated position at the table easily enough. Thomas' voice called out, then, sounding subdued and defeated.

"We've only a few crusts of bread to go around; take no more than your ration, and then pass the basket down to the next man."

His voice took on more of its old strength, and he added, "Just because old Gad thinks us savages doesn't mean that we need to prove him right. Take your share and no more, and everyone will get something to eat."

Nobody replied, and Alec could feel the basket slide down the table into his hands. Inside, he found a few loaves of stale bread still in the bottom, and one with an end broken off. He tore off no more than a couple of inches from the loaf, and wordlessly pushed the basket on to the next man.

He bit off a mouthful of the bread, and wished at once that there had been beer or cider provided with it. It was dry and tasted as though the unknown baker had been too free with the salt, which probably explained why they had been given it at all. On the positive side of the ledger, it did seem to be fresher than he'd supposed; it had only felt stale because the surplus of salt had restrained the barm from raising the dough correctly.

One of the consequences of growing up without sisters was that Alec had been given the duty of helping his mother in the kitchen from time to time, so he had more than a passing familiarity with the ways in which bread could be spoiled by an incautious baker.

As he was still musing on these memories, the last of his bread long since chewed and mechanically swallowed, he and the rest of the prisoners were blinded by the appearance of bright light cast down the entrance shaft.

Gad called ahead of himself, "I warn you, I am still armed, as are the others with me. Do not think to try anything."

None of the men sitting around the table, blinking in the unaccustomed brightness reflected from the rocks at the end of the room, seemed inclined to do any such thing, Alec thought, but he only frowned.

In the growing light, as the guards came closer in their descent down the ladder, Alec could see the dull looks of resignation on most of the other men's faces. The exceptions were Thomas, who looked resolute, and Charles, whose rage was contained, but only for the moment, and only out of utter necessity.

Gad appeared, holding a torch over his head, flanked by two other guards, who had both drawn their pistols and held them leveled on the prisoners, as though certain that some one of their number would take the opportunity to revolt.

Alec suppressed the urge to giggle at the thought of these beaten men doing any such thing.

"Listen well, and do not think to interrupt or ask questions," Gad said imperiously. "Jonas has been dismissed as the head of our guard, and I have been appointed in his place. I will, naturally, be leading the inquiry into the events that led to the death of your companion. With the recent disorder, we will not be permitting any above-ground activities for the time being, until we can establish some means of ensuring your safe conduct.

"I will be undertaking interrogations to determine the truth of what happened here, and how it led to the murder of one of your number. As I warned you would happen last night, once I have identified the culprit responsible for taking the prisoner's life, I have been authorized to employ the penalty of death for the killer."

He permitted himself a satisfied smirk, adding, "Any who help to shield the perpetrator will, of course, be subject to the stock and whip, and I may even be allowed the use of more direct means to stimulate your honest recall of events."

He gestured toward the empty basket. "Your rations will be reduced to bread and water until the inquiry is concluded, and as water is available in abundance down here, it hardly seems sensible to raise it from the well, carry it all the way over to the guardhouse, and then lower it down to you, when all you need to do is cup your hands below one of the ready sources and drink your fill."

He nodded brusquely. "That is all."

He turned and said quietly to one of the guards, a slight young man who appeared to be scarcely older than Alec had been when he'd joined the militia, "Go and get the litter; we've a corpse to bring aboveground."

The day was divided between utter boredom and moments of terror. Accustomed as they were to hard labor in the sunlight and springtime air, being locked back into the unrelieved darkness and increasingly ripe stench of a small chamber full of frightened men had an effect on the prisoners beyond nearly any torture that Gad might be able to devise.

While they waited for whatever was to come next, Thomas spoke quietly into the gloom. "If you are chosen for questioning, tell all; we have nothing left to hide from him, and while the truth we have to share is not the truth he seeks, it has the benefit of being easy for each of us to remember relatively clearly."

The only answer was a guttural bark of a chuckle from Charles. "You lot may not have anything left to hide, but I still have hope for escape, by any means I may be able to devise, and

I'll not be so foolish as to give our jailers advance warning of that fact."

Thomas answered with a solemn tone in his voice, "Nor would I expect you to. Only regarding those events which have already passed need we agree to speak only the truth."

Charles did not answer.

It seemed to Alec that it was not long after that when Gad threw open the iron door, admitting a tiny sliver of light and the sound of his voice, cold and determined. "Charles McIntosh, stand forth for questioning. You may climb the ladder, unaccompanied, but know that I have my pistol drawn, loaded, and ready for use, should you try any mischief."

After Charles climbed up, the door banged closed again, the light was extinguished, and Alec could hear the heavy bolt slide into place, ensuring that the door could not be opened again from underneath.

After Charles returned and went back to his bunk without saying a word, the pattern was set for the rest of the day. Every so often, the door at the top of the shaft would clang open, and Gad or one of his deputies would shout a name, and one of their number would start up suddenly from his bunk, usually with the sound of a sharp gasp of fear audible to everyone.

By the time the summoned man was ready to ascend, the prior subject of Gad's interrogation would be climbing down the ladder, sometimes silent, and sometimes uttering little cries of pain as he moved back to his bunk, evidence of the brutality of whatever had passed aboveground. None spoke upon his return, which added an even more ominous note to the already thick silence underground.

Alec spent most of the day listening to an intermittent drip of water somewhere down the tunnel. It was not a steady pattern, but irregular, sometimes seeming as though an hour passed from one drop to the next, and sometimes barely a handful of minutes. Such was the lack of external indicators of time's progress that he questioned whether it might not have been as steady as the beat of a drum leading men on a march, and it was only a failure of his perception that gave the impression of infrequency.

He lay in anticipation of the next drop when the iron door clanged open again, and Gad shouted down, "Alexander Tinsworth, stand forth for questioning."

In spite of himself, Alec's heart began to pound, and he rose as silently as the rest had done, walking toward the patch of light spilling on the rock beneath the mine shaft.

The last man who had been questioned – Daniel – was nearly to the bottom of the ladder, and Alec waited for the thief to pass him. He wondered idly whether the man had disclosed the coin he presumably still held somewhere on his person, but decided that he would say nothing of it himself unless Gad should ask.

Daniel reached the bottom of the ladder, and Alec gasped to see that the man's face was scraped and bruised, one eye swollen shut already. Daniel avoided meeting Alec's gaze with his one good eye, and scurried down into the darkness as though he was now frightened not of the dark, like most men, but of the light.

Alec gulped back his fear and started climbing, the light at the top of the mine shaft beckoning him, though he was reminded forcefully of a moth he'd once watched fly directly into the flame of a candle, to its destruction, and he wondered whether a similar fate awaited him in the light of day.

At the door, Gad waited with his hand resting on the butt of his pistol. He had removed both his jacket and his waistcoat, leaving him looking as though he were a common laborer, although an uncommonly well-armed one. As Alec emerged into the brightly-lit kitchen, blinking away the darkness, Gad took hold of his arm firmly enough to bring tears to Alec's eyes.

"Come this way, prisoner."

They sat at Jonas' old desk, and Gad flipped over a sheet of paper, dipping his quill. "Mister Tinsworth, you will begin by telling me what you know of James Cadwaller's untimely demise."

"Aye, sir."

Alec laid out what he had heard and then what he'd seen, sparing no detail.

Gad asked sharply, "And the rock that you believe fell onto Mister Cadwaller's head came from the old ore shaft?"

"Aye sir, it appeared to have done."

Gad's mouth pursed unpleasantly. "But you were not present, and did not see the rock fall, nor even hear it?"

"Nay, as I said, I only became aware of it as word was passed down the line, and then saw it after Thomas fetched a light."

"Do you know who was working at the entrance to the ore shaft when Mister Cadwaller was killed?"

"Why, no, sir, not with any certainty. Thomas and Charles had said that they would take that duty, so as not to ask anyone else to expose themselves to the hazards of... well, of what happened."

Gad scratched a line of text onto the page, and Alec wished that he could read what the man had written. "Do you think that Charles McIntosh is capable of committing an act of murder?"

Alec hadn't expected that question, and his brow furrowed

as he considered how to answer.

In truth, he did believe that Charles was capable of committing murder — indeed, he'd bragged of killing Patriots in a variety of lurid manners. But was there any chance that he could have committed the murder of his friend?

Alec had to stammer, "I-I am not certain, sir."

Gad's quill scratched on the page again, then fell still. "What of Thomas Effingham?"

This time, Alec had no uncertainty. "No, sir, I cannot picture Thomas hurting anyone of our company."

Gad looked at him through narrowed eyes. "And if he thought a man not to be of your company?"

Alec recalled the way that Thomas had described the fate of the informer, and he frowned. "I know not whether he could be driven to act against someone who was opposing our cause, outside of a field of battle, but I do not believe that he would, no."

Gad nodded, his mouth pressed into a grim line, revealing nothing. "Has anyone in your company spoken of causing the deaths of other prisoners, past or future?"

"Not directly, sir, no."

Gad frowned, but did not follow up on that line of questioning, instead moving on. "Who of your number originated the plot to escape through the ore shaft?"

Alec swallowed hard, but remembered Thomas' instructions. "It was Mister Effingham's idea, sir, though he was seeking to improve upon Mister McIntosh's original intent to tunnel out through raw rock. Mister McIntosh seemed insensible to the warning that others have died in the past by attempting to escape by this means, and so Mister Effingham offered it as an alternative that he thought safer."

Gad gave a snort, and wrote again for a moment. After a decent silence, he commented, "I suppose future prisoners will know better than to suggest this escape, now, too." He looked up, and his eyes held Alec's fixed in a long, hard gaze before he asked, "And if you had escaped, where would you have flown?"

Again, Alec was caught off-guard by Gad's line of questioning. "I know not, sir."

Gad snorted, and Alec could see the man's fist clenching, reminding him what the guard had done to Daniel. "Surely, the thought of departing from this place by one means or another has occurred to you. Where will you go, should you depart of your own accord?"

Afraid that the truth — being that he had no idea — would not satisfy Gad, Alec finally said, "Why, I suppose, to my father."

Even as he said the words, he realized that they were true, and that he would hope that his father could arrange a meeting with Miss Landry afterward.

Gad wrote a final note, and then stood. "Very well, Mister Tinsworth, you may return to your quarters until you are again summoned. You may not speak to anyone below of the questions I have put to you here, on pain of the severest punishment. Follow me."

Alec stood, understanding now why the other prisoners who'd been questioned had said nothing of their experience on their return. What he did not understand was why Gad had been so easy on him. He'd expected to be beaten, and possibly made to endure outright torture.

Gad threw open the iron door with the customary clang —

far louder at this proximity than it was from the chamber below —
and consulted his notes before he called down, "Henry Lipscombe,
stand forth for questioning."

He nodded toward the door, and Alec began the climb
down toward the safety of the mine, happy to be out of reach of the
guard and his unpredictable temper.

Chapter 20

At some point in the cycle of questioning, Alec had fallen asleep, so he did not notice when it came to an end, and only jerked back into consciousness with the normal pots-and-pans banging clangor from the top of the shaft.

"Bread and water as before," Gad's voice echoed down. "No candles, no comforts." His cold chuckle sounded. "Pass the day as you see fit."

Alec was far from the only one to groan as he stood up from his bunk, and the sounds of the other men moving tentatively toward the mine shaft or the tables were painful and tentative. Alec sat at the end of the bench, waiting wearily for the bread to make its way down to him.

Beside him, he heard another man sit down, his movements tentative, almost furtive. The man let out a small cry of pain as he swung his leg over the bench and it collided with Alec's side, and Alec recognized Daniel's voice.

"So sorry, sir, 'twas an accident, thought I had room," Daniel said with desperate quiet.

"It's all right, Daniel," Alec said. "I'm not hurt, as you weren't moving quickly."

"Oh, 'tis you," Daniel said, sounding, if anything, even more obeisant and miserable.

"Not to worry, friend." Alec paused, wondering if the prior

day's command against speaking of their ordeals at Gad's hands was still in effect. "Are you hurt badly?"

Daniel replied, the weakness of his voice at odds with his words, "Nay, not so badly as all of that. 'Tis but the ill effects of my own great clumsiness, before any other cause."

Alec frowned, aware that his expression would communicate nothing without light to make it visible. "I do not understand what he hoped to learn by hurting men," he said. "With nothing but the unchanging truth given to him by all our number, he must soon have realized that there was no murder, only an accident in the commission of a different crime."

Daniel chuckled, though it sounded wheezing and strained. "Even had there been no death, do you think that he would have hesitated to heap injury on those members of our party who he suspected of involvement in the escape plan? Or on those, like myself, who he thought he could get further information from?"

Alec thought that he heard a note of pride in Daniel's voice as he continued.

"He may have thought that he could crack me, get me to give him more information than I already had about the escape plan, but I done gave it to him all from the very start, so he became quite frustrated with me, which led me directly to... being clumsy aboveground."

Alec felt almost sorry for the thief, hearing him cling to some shred of his pride over such a small matter as refraining from making up whatever Daniel thought that Gad might like to hear, never mind casting suspicion on some other member of the party to spare himself.

As base a creature as Daniel might be, as low as his fortunes may have ebbed, it somehow did Alec's heart some good to hear that there were some things that the thief wasn't willing to stoop to.

Rather than argue with the other man over the severity and causes of his injuries, Alec instead simply said, "Thank you," and left it at that.

Another man's voice, Charles', rumbled from the darkness at the other end of the table. "That one, Gad, he seems to just like hurting people. Long after he'd gotten what he wanted from me, and I'd told him truthfully all I knew, he continued to beat me as though he thought I was concealing something from him."

Thomas spoke up now, his calm demeanor still evident in his tone, despite a new raspiness that Alec had never noticed from him before. "Gad has long been frustrated with what he believed to be a lack of appropriate discipline over us prisoners. Now that he has achieved his aim of gaining the whip hand, so to speak, over this gaol, he means to wield it, and frequently."

Charles growled, "I'll not put up with it another hour longer than I must, and I will mark him for vengeance, come the day that their absurd rebellion is put down once and for all."

"When our friends and neighbors who have sided with the doomed cause of independency finally come to see the futility of their project, our most important aim must be to make them see that they are subjects of a just and benevolent King," Thomas said, his voice sounding harsh and angry through the hoarseness with which he'd been gifted during his excursion aboveground.

He continued, his tone slightly gentler, but no less firm, "Vengeance will only beget vengeance, and the war will never come to a decisive end. Magnanimity in our victory will ensure that it remains a solid and permanent thing. Yes, there have been acts of barbarity committed against His Majesty's forces and allies on these shores, but we must be the ones to stand up and say that these are not the acts of civilized men, but those of animals seeking only the satisfaction of their basest urges — and we must choose civilization over satisfaction."

Alec felt sure that he could hear Thomas breathing hard after this oration, and he could not resist the urge to slap a palm on the table, crying out, "Hear, hear!" as he'd been told the men of Parliament often did. He was only slightly surprised when he realized that he had not been the only one to react this way.

Charles sneered, "Pretty speeches do not deliver the justice they deserve to the men who have committed the worst of the offenses against our persons and our friends. Men such as our jailers ought be brought before a magistrate, evidence presented against them, where they may then be judged guilty or innocent, and finally served with the swift application of the gallows when their guilt has been established to the satisfaction of the judge."

He spat, the sound somehow conveying more disrespect in the darkness than in normal conversation. "Since we've no magistrate in these parts, nor any functioning system of law, it is our rightful duty to deliver this justice at our own hands, when and where we are able."

"No," Thomas countered immediately, before Charles could even complete the development of his argument. "I have heard stories of this sort of justice being dispensed by men on both sides, but I have never yet heard of a case where it achieved what ought to be the overriding goal — to restore those injured by injustice to their prior state."

"Nay, 'tis to stop evildoers from hurting further victims," Charles shot back. "There is no justice in merely restoring stolen property to the victim of a thief, if the thief is unhindered in his ability to steal again."

Alec could hear Daniel shifting uncomfortably beside him.

Charles pounded on the table for emphasis, an explosion of sound that made Alec jump. "No, the thief must serve time in a gaol to instruct him on the error of his ways, and the traitor must swing on the gallows to discourage treachery in the actions of his fellows."

Thomas' tone was now more one of sadness as he said simply, "'Tis treachery, but against a different claim of legitimate government, for which we are at present confined under the earth. I think it a good thing that our jailers do not fully share your vision for the most effective way to persuade wrong-doers, considering how they see us, and the error of our ways."

Charles made a disgusted noise, but did not otherwise continue to pursue the argument.

Alec felt the basket of bread shoved into his hands, and he reached into it, finding nothing but a jaggedly torn-off heel in one corner of the container. He sighed and retrieved it, finding it hard and stale against his teeth. Where were their jailers finding a continuous supply of such inedible bread?

He was still chewing and pondering this question when the door at the entrance shaft banged open again, and Gad's voice boomed down.

"Alec Tinsworth, stand forth for a visitor."

Alec started at the sound of his name from Gad's mouth for the second time in two days, but dutifully stood, though he could not imagine what visitor could have overcome Gad's clear prohibition on any form of comforts for the prisoners.

As he walked down the length of the table, Charles hissed, "Wait a moment. This is our opportunity, and the like will not be presented again in any predictable amount of time."

He laid out a plan of action in swift, decisive words, overriding Thomas' objections with a curt, "We tried it your way. Now we try mine."

Gad's voice boomed down the mine's entrance shaft a second time. "Alexander Tinsworth, stand forth for a visitor, or we shall be forced to send her back whither she came."

Alec's heart leapt into his throat. It had to be Miss Landry, come to visit him in the prison, apparently without either her father or his.

Before he could wonder further at the meaning of this visit, Charles was beside him, his whisper deafening in Alec's ear. "Answer him, you fool. Tell him you will be but a moment."

Alec called up the mine shaft, "I beg of you, give me a moment to put on clothing, sir, as I was yet undressed for sleep."

Charles whispered, "Good, good. Now gather the rest at the bottom of the ladder, as our moment will only be a short one, if it comes at all. When I give the signal, stand ready to climb quickly, as if your very life depends on it. Are you clear on our purpose?"

Alec, his heart now pounding against his ribcage for escape, answered simply, "Aye." Then he stood and made his way toward the dim light leaking down through the bars in the iron door at the top of the mine shaft.

Charles started up the ladder ahead of him, and Alec heard the other men moving to stand behind him. Daniel bumped into his back, muttering a quiet, "Excuse me, sir," as they waited for Charles' signal from the top of the shaft.

When he reached the top of the ladder, Charles rapped at the inside of the door impatiently. Alec saw the door start to open, and then several things happened all at once.

Gad's face appeared at the edge of the door, and Alec saw his eyes go wide as he recognized Charles at the door. Charles' hand shot out and grabbed Gad's hand from the edge of the door, pulling him away from it to prevent the guard from re-closing it. Gad gave a strangled yelp and was suddenly falling down the shaft, his yelp changing into a full-throated bellow. Alec stood transfixed as the guard fell directly down the shaft toward him.

Something hit Alec from behind, and he was aware of a dull whumph of air being forced out of lungs as the mass of Gad's body struck something behind him, silencing the guard's roar in an instant.

Alec spun around and saw, under the guard's inert body, another still form – that of the thief, Daniel, who had sacrificed himself to keep Alec from being crushed by the falling man.

He had no time to ponder the shock of the sudden sequence of events, though, as Charles shouted down, "That was the signal, you fools! Climb now!"

Without conscious thought, Alec reached for the ladder and watched himself ascend the rungs, almost as if it were someone else's arms and legs performing the rote motions of swarming up to the surface. At the top, standing in almost blinding radiance, was Miss Landry, her mouth hanging open in stunned horror at what she had just witnessed.

Still operating on unthinking instinct, Alec grabbed the

girl's hand and followed Charles out of the guardhouse and toward the main gate of the prison walls. A guard looked up in sleepy surprise as Charles and Alec appeared at the gate, Miss Landry still in tow, and other prisoners streaming out of the guardhouse behind them.

Charles stopped and spoke decisively to the guard. "There's something wrong in the mine, and Gad told us all to get out. I think he's hurt – go help him. I'll hold your position here until help can arrive."

The guard, his eyes wide with fright at the sudden, unexpected appearance of so many prisoners moving toward him, nodded, and seemed ready to accept commands from anyone, if it only freed him from the responsibility of making a decision himself.

As soon as the frightened man started running toward the guardhouse, Charles slid the bolt in the prison gate and pulled the door open, leaving nothing between Alec and the world without for the first time in months.

Almost in a daze, he stepped toward the gate, only to be restrained by Miss Landry, who planted her feet, her eyes wide in disbelief.

"Do you mean to simply leave?"

Charles answered for Alec. "No, miss, we mean to escape. Get gone," he tossed over his shoulder at Alec, even as he started running for the forest himself.

Alec gave Miss Landry's hand another tug, and she came along this time. Maybe not eagerly, but she followed as he picked up speed, heading for a dark path he'd spotted opening up into the undergrowth that lay beneath the trees that crowded close about the road leading to the prison.

After they had run together for a while, they lost sight of the other prisoners as they fanned out into the woods themselves, singly or in groups. Alec and Miss Landry came into a small clearing, deeply shaded, but opening up enough for them to stop and catch their breath.

It wasn't until then that Alec let go of the girl's hand, and as he stood panting, hands on his knees, to try to catch his breath, he looked up at her.

Her face shone with her effort, and he couldn't help but notice a bead of sweat trickling out from under her mob cap, making its way down her temple. She was looking back at him, her expression of shock turning to one that portended dismay and anger.

When she could speak, she repeated, "Do you mean to simply leave, abandoning a guard to die, and your fellow prisoners to their own fates? Will you not be snatched up by the militia in the country around within a matter of hours, with a murder on your name, in addition to the charge of escape? Where do you mean to go, and how do you plan to avoid discovery?"

She stopped to take a breath again, and he held up a hand, still breathing heavily himself. "I confess, I had no plan beyond the walls that I have now escaped, other than seeking your society and my father's, and leaving to him what was to be done next."

Miss Landry gaped at him. "My society? Am I to believe that you escaped from prison for the purpose of coming to me, though we know each other but slightly, regardless of what designs our fathers may have for us?"

Alec felt his face go hot, and he knew that he must be as red as a beet. "A-aye," he stammered. "I meant at least to speak to you of the designs that our fathers had for us, and learn whether those designs might be worthy of pursuit."

She favored him with a half-smile before her expression returned to one of intense thought. Finally, she answered, "Now is not the moment for seeking answers to those questions, though I do appreciate your forthrightness. At the present moment, we need to put our efforts toward making good your escape, and ensuring that you do not fall back into the hands of the rebels under any circumstances."

She shook her head at him, that same enigmatic smile passing across her face as she did so. She said, almost more to herself than to him, "One reads of men performing all manner of feats in pursuit of women, but those are supposed to be fabulists' tales, not the acts of real men."

She laughed suddenly. "Will my father now ask you to go and collect the golden fleece in the company of Jason's Argonauts?"

Alec gave her a look of complete incomprehension, and she waved away the questions already forming on his face, laughing anew. "It's something my tutor made me read in practicing Greek. I don't know why it came to my mind."

Alec closed his mouth, and considered Miss Landry. When she'd laughed, it seemed as though her face had changed into that of a different girl's, and what had looked plain to him before struck him as endearing.

He shook his head, dispelling the thought even as it occurred to him that this was exactly what his father had advised him to seek in her visage.

Her expression grew serious again, though, and she said, "I

rode one of my father's horses to the gaol, but it is not a good idea to go back and claim it now, or perhaps ever. The road from my home is not a terribly long ride, but it would be a difficult walk to complete before the sun goes down, even if we could use the roads."

She gave him a glance of appraisal, taking in his ragged clothing and ill-fitting, if solid, shoes. "Do you know the country about here at all?"

"Nay," he answered. "I was taken into captivity a couple of days' march from here, but I was brought in under guard and in no condition to take note of my path hence."

She nodded, grimacing. "I didn't expect that you would, but I thought I'd ask. I do not know this area, either, nor do I possess much of the arts of living rough." She squared her shoulders. "Well, there's nothing to be done for it, and a hungry day never ended anyone. Can you point us toward the west, at least?"

Alec looked up, frowning at the few patches of springtime sun they could see through the new leaves of the crowns of the trees around them. "I know not the hour, as we have been held underground for a span of days, and our routine was irregular as a result."

She answered quickly, "It should be coming up on midday, as I left my house after breaking my fast, and it does not take more than a couple of hours to ride the distance. I do not think it likely that the afternoon will have advanced very far, in any event."

He frowned again. "It would be better for this purpose if it were, as at least the sun would lead us in the direction you need." He thought hard for a moment. "Earlier in the season, it would be easier to tell south, at least, as the sun would stay close to that horizon all day."

He looked at her and shrugged. "Between the two, and what I can see of it through the trees, the sun is relatively near to the zenith at the moment, though I think it favors that direction." He pointed to the left of the path they had followed to the clearing.

Inclining his head that way, he said, "I think, therefore, that we were going westward before, and can continue that way until the sun gives us a more definite indication."

She crossed her arms over her chest. "If I weren't worried about guards coming out this far in search of escapees, I would argue for staying here until we had a better sense of our direction, but under the circumstances, it is better to move in a wrong direction than to remain stationary." She gestured toward the path. "Lead the way. This is your escape, after all."

They proceeded through the woods, following the winding animal track that led out of the clearing. Alec did his best to keep an accounting of the various turns they took, but he found that the glimpses of the sun through the dense canopy of the trees was a more reliable guide to their progress.

He was glad for Miss Landry's quiet, determined pace following him, although he found that he was glancing back frequently to ensure that she was still behind him. However, most of the time, he had only to focus on finding the path through the thick undergrowth. This left him plenty of time to ponder what had just happened to lead to the shocking transition from sharing the claustrophobic confines of the underground chamber with a score or more of men, to moving through a path rendered nearly as close by the shrubs and branches of the forest.

Never mind the substantial differences between Miss Landry's company and that of his fellow prisoners. His mind shied away from that overwhelming thought as though burned, though, and returned to going over his confused final moments in the darkness.

He was coming to the realization that Daniel was likely dead, along with Gad, and that the thief had given his life to save him from being struck by Gad's falling body. To have purchased his salvation for the price of an unearned coin was more than he could bear to think of for long.

He said a quick prayer for the thief's tarnished soul as he darted forward under a low branch, looking back to make sure that it didn't strike Miss Landry in the face as she followed.

The fact that she was following him was another act taken on his behalf that he could not immediately understand. She could have parted ways with him anywhere along their headlong flight from the prison — she could still, with a completely clear conscience— and yet, she seemed dedicated to ensuring that he made it to safety, without concern for any cost to her reputation or safety.

Ahead, he saw more light breaking through the forest, and soon enough, they found themselves at the edge of the wooded region, looking over a broad valley of fields. A lone, low farmhouse was visible in the distance, smoke curling up peacefully in the springtime air.

Miss Landry came up beside Alec, staring intently at the scene before them. Her brow furrowed, and she said, "I think that I may have passed that house on my way to the prison. It is hard to know from this angle, though. If I am right, the road is just on the other side."

She shrugged and gestured at the sun, which hung high over the far side of the valley. "In any event, it looks as though we are still facing west, so that is a positive thing. However, I do not think that it would be prudent to expose ourselves to any eye that might glance this way by proceeding through the open fields, so I think we'll have to follow the edge of the forest that way."

She pointed to the south, where the trees massed over a rough stone fence line at the edge of cleared ground, some of which was freshly plowed, making ready for the planting season.

Though they had just passed through that same forest, Alec could not help but feel a prickle of fear run down his spine at its ominous appearance from this vantage.

He nodded in reply to her. "I agree that to be visible from any distance whatever would be an act of foolishness, as the alarm may not yet have reached this far, but anyone reporting strangers in the land, on seeing us, could well lead to my recapture." He grimaced, looking at the edge of the forest.

"In fact, I wonder whether merely sticking to the verge is sufficient to keep us out of view. If there are paths that might lead us just inside the edge of the forest, they might serve our purposes better."

He saw Miss Landry suppress a delicate shudder, and he realized anew what the passage through the forest must have cost her. He looked her over more carefully, and saw that her mob cap had been pulled half-off by some grasping branch, and the hem of her skirts was caked in mud and had twigs caught in the frayed edges of one side. There was a welt along the line of her chin where he must have caught her with a released bough as he passed through, and her boots looked to be completely ruined by the small creek they had forded along the way.

He said abruptly, "Never mind that, on second thought.

Let us proceed along the verge, and seek what cover we can find along the way, but the hazards of the forest are likely greater than those of the path along its edge."

She seemed to relax visibly as she said, "That sounds like a good idea, though if we see a soul, we ought stand ready to take refuge in the forest."

Alec shot Miss Landry a grateful smile and had turned to go in the direction they'd agreed on, when he heard a distant report, the sound of either a musket or a pistol at some range.

He glanced sharply around, Miss Landry frozen behind him, and thought that the sound had come from somewhere behind them, or even from the prison itself, on the far side of the forest.

Miss Landry took a step closer to him and whispered, "Do you think they saw us?"

"Nay, 'twas no place near us. Either in the forest or beyond it."

He pursed his mouth as he considered. The shot may have been from a pursuer, or it may have even been something completely unrelated, but it was the first evidence that they might be actively pursued. Their track had to be relatively easy to see in the woods, and it would lead anyone looking for escaped prisoners straight to them.

He glanced in the direction of the farmhouse. He saw nobody in evidence there, but he could not be certain there wasn't someone behind its windows, observing them even now.

He steeled his nerve. It was a chance that they'd have to take.

"Here," he said, walking toward the stone fence and stepping up onto it. He held out a hand to her, and she followed him up onto the roughly laid stones.

On some farms, Alec knew, the farmers would take great pride in dressing and laying the stones into careful and stable fences, built to last generations. On others, though, the farmers simply gathered the stones that appeared on the surface with the springtime plowing, and piled them at the edge of their land to get them out of the way.

The top layer of the stones they stepped onto now still had mud clinging to them in places, and this farm was definitely of the minimalist school of thought in their approach to fence-building.

Carefully, Alec stepped forward along the top of the heaped stones, saying over his shoulder to Miss Landry, "This will make us harder to track, but we'll need to mind our step. Once we've broken our trail sufficiently, we can come back down off the stone."

She replied, delight in her voice, "I would never have thought of that, Mister Tinsworth. It seems that you are clever enough to manage an escape in spite of it coming as a surprise to you."

He grinned at her over his shoulder, but said nothing, putting his energy instead into the task of finding solid footing. He'd step onto a rock, feel it shift under his foot, and step back to find another that was more ready to take his weight. Other times, he'd feel a rock slide away under his foot after he'd committed himself to it, and need to leap to another.

Miss Landry seemed to be having an easier time of it, lightly and deftly moving along the fence, making it look to Alec as though she were traveling on a cobbled street. He grimaced as a rock tilted forward suddenly under him, pitching him with it and forcing him to mill his arms wildly to remain standing long enough to reach the next step.

He heard a delicate laugh behind him, and though he wanted to glare at Miss Landry for making sport of him, when he looked back at her, the transformation had again overtaken her face, turning it into a work of no small beauty, in his estimation. Beyond her, he could see that they'd come a couple hundred yards from the tree that marked the outlet of the path through the woods.

"I think we can safely come down from the fence now," he said, and stepped carefully down the heaped rock to the side nearer the woods. "If we stay behind the fence line, it will give us some cover from the open fields, and provide a handy place to hide, should we see anyone out there who might spy us."

Miss Landry followed him down, taking his offered hand to make the final steps to level ground, and fell against him as her momentum carried her off the last rock.

His arm shot around her waist to steady her, until he awkwardly snatched it away, as though burned.

He could feel his face flush warm as he muttered an apology, which inexplicably triggered another smile from Miss Landry.

Turning away, he peered down the fence line, noting that there appeared to be enough clear space between it and the edge of the forest for them to move along pretty briskly now.

"Come on, let us be off," he said, and started walking briskly away, only glancing back long enough to assure himself that she was following.

Chapter 21

Alec peered down the gently curving stone fence, shielding his eyes from the setting sun, which shone directly in his face. Behind him, Miss Landry still marched gamely a l o n g , though he had noticed that she was limping, and his own feet ached as though they'd been crushed under carriage wheels.

It was hard to believe that he could have grown so soft in just a couple of months' time, but the amount of walking he'd been able to do during his captivity had pretty well been limited to a few dozen yards in any direction.

"We'll have to stop for the night and find someplace to rest," he said over his shoulder, and Miss Landry nodded grimly.

"I was not sensible of the distance I had ridden to come to you. It looks so easy when the horse is putting the miles behind itself."

Alec grunted agreement, though he had little enough experience with riding. He'd ridden occasionally growing up, though that had been his brother's interest far more than his. Then, after joining the militia, he had marched everywhere, which was part of what led him to be so surprised at the hardship that a short day's walk was causing him.

A passing breeze plucked at his threadbare shirt, and he shivered at the chill it brought with it. Springtime in Connecticut was sweet in the daytime, but was hardly suitable to sleeping rough through the night. He didn't suppose that Miss Landry had any means of sparking a fire, and for the first time, he wondered whether he might not make it back to his father at all.

He was keeping an eye out for a suitable place for them to rest for the night, and didn't notice at first that Miss Landry was no longer right behind him. He glanced back to ask her something, and stopped dead in his tracks.

She was nowhere to be seen.

Breaking into a run, he retraced his steps until he saw her sitting propped against the stone fence, sobbing quietly. He watched her for a moment, unsure what to do.

Approaching her more slowly, he asked in a helpless tone, "Whatever is the matter, Miss Landry?"

She could not answer immediately, but eventually mastered herself enough to hiccup out, "I—I—had no idea—it would be—so difficult. I thought—we would walk—no longer than—the dinner hour— but, it seems—it seems—oh!" She buried her face in her hands, her shoulders again quaking as she cried.

Not knowing what else to do, Alec sat down beside her and put his arm around her, pulling her over so that her head could rest on his shoulder. She clutched at him with the desperation of a drowning man, and wept until there was nothing left but short, hiccupping breaths, and Alec's shoulder was soaked right through.

As if by instinct, he stroked her hair where it had escaped from her mob cap, and murmured, "We'll be all right. All will turn out in the end, just you wait and see."

She said nothing, but her breathing gradually slowed and became even, until he realized that she had fallen asleep, half-cradled in his arm. He couldn't help but notice that she was warm, where her side pressed against his, and he allowed himself to relax into the rock wall behind him, thanking his good fortune that it was smooth enough to do so.

His free hand rested in what remained of the prior autumn's leaves, and he flexed his fingers slightly to ward off the chill of the earth beneath them. His head came to rest atop hers, and his last conscious thought as he drifted off to sleep was that her hair smelled somehow of sunshine, and it tickled his nose ever so slightly.

A rustling in the leaves woke him with a start, and the pale, evenly-graduated purple of the sky beyond the edge of the woods portended another day of glorious blue dawning soon. Miss Landry stirred at his jump in reaction to the noise of what he could now see was a chipmunk, advancing in short bursts along the verge of the woods. She sat up, disentangling her limbs from his, and looked at him for a long moment, and it was as though he could see the memory of the prior day flooding back into her mind.

She sighed and smiled faintly. "I suppose that you made a better pillow for me than the rock did for you."

He smiled involuntarily in response, the arm she'd been sleeping on suddenly coming alive with the prickling sensation of hot needles all over his skin. He grimaced through his smile, replying, "I hope so, as I hope that you slept at least as well as I?"

"I remember nothing after you sat beside me," she said, "until this moment. I suppose that walking for half the day without break will do that to most anyone."

She grimaced then, her fingers resting on her stomach. "Speaking of needing a break, I must find a place to attend to my needs. I shall return in a trice."

He nodded, standing and stretching, trying to work some of

the stiffness out of his joints. Though he may have been accustomed to sleeping in cold, with little in the way of a blanket for warmth, the chill from the ground seemed to have seeped straight into his bones.

Miss Landry returned, clutching a double handful of greens. "Look at what I found! Ramps, just ready to eat." She held them up for Alec to see, and his stomach lurched in hunger. As she came closer, he caught the pungent odor of the woodland treat, and his mouth started watering.

"That is a lucky stroke indeed," he said, eagerly accepting the cluster she offered him. He separated one plant out of the bunch and barely bothered to brush the soil off of the bulb at the bottom of the leaves before biting into it, smiling widely.

She followed suit with one of her own, and returned his grin. She wrinkled her nose, saying, "I think they may be a bit past their prime, but they are far better than nothing."

"Oh, aye," he said. "It has been two years and more since I've had a ramp. Why, my mother used to..." He trailed off, struck suddenly by the weight of the fact that he would never again have ramps the way she prepared them, nor anything else, either.

He took another bite to cover his reaction, and closed his eyes as he chewed, until he could manage to open them without letting loose the tears that threatened to spill over. When he did, he found Miss Landry gazing at him sympathetically, and her hand came to rest on his shoulder to comfort him.

"I know, Alec," she said softly. "Your mother's passing was a great shock to us all." Her hand squeezed his shoulder gently before she released it.

He looked at her with gratitude for her understanding, but said nothing.

She peered down the line of the fence then, declaring, "I do believe I know that house."

Alec followed her gaze, and saw the structure she was looking at. It stood only a short distance from the wall, and appeared at this distance to be little more than a rude shack, built of rough-hewn logs.

"How do you know it?"

"Why, 'tis the Jameson house, if I don't miss my guess," she said. "He's no friend of the Tories in the district, so we'll need to conceal ourselves in order to pass, but I know well how his property is situated in relation to my father's. We are no more than an hour's walk from home when we reach it."

He squared his shoulders and gestured for her to take the lead. "Then let us be on our way, and perhaps we can finish breaking our fast around your own table, rather than in the woods." He took another bite of ramp, adding hastily, "Not that I object to eating what you so cleverly found for us."

She smiled in acknowledgment of his near gaffe, and took another bite herself as she swung into motion, moving off into the woods with Alec following behind her.

By the time the sun had cleared the edge of the forest to warm their backs, she was pointing out landmarks and hurrying from one to the next. "Not far now," she said, leading him up onto the road at last. "Just around this next bend."

They rounded the bend, and she skidded to a stop, then darted behind a tree, hauling Alec by the hand. She crouched down, peering around the edge of the tree, and hissed to him, "There is a strange horse tied up out front, as well as my father's horse that I rode to the prison. While it may be a simple matter of someone returning the horse, I fear that the gaol guard or even the militia may be here seeking after you."

He risked a peek himself, and saw a pair of horses picketed in front of a modest, well-kept house.

"What will we do?"

Her answer was grim and determined. "We wait. Once my father's caller has departed, we can see whether the house remains any refuge at all." She moved down a slight slope into a clump of overgrown grass, which shielded them from both the house and the road.

Alec moved down to sit beside her, taking her hand in a reassuring gesture. She favored him with a tight, nervous smile. It seemed to Alec as though they'd sat that way for an hour before they finally heard the steady clop of a horse being ridden away.

Miss Landry crept up to where she could rise into a low crouch to see, leaving Alec in the grass, and then stood up fully, motioning for him to follow her.

"He is gone," she said, and together, they walked the short way to the house.

Just before they reached the front porch, the door opened, and Alec's father stepped out, saying to someone still inside, "I hope they have the sense to go elsewhere, but I'm glad to know they haven't yet been captured." As he pulled the door closed, he turned to face outside, and his jaw dropped.

Alec rushed forward into his father's arms, and father and son shared a long, wordless embrace.

Finally, his father stepped back, looking Alec in the eye. "This is the last place you should have come, but I am very glad you are here."

Chapter 22

Sitting at Mister Landry's table was somewhat surreal for Alec.

After gathering his daughter into his arms, apparently stricken dumb with worry, Mister Landry had led them into the kitchen, saying, "When Mister Garrick of the gaol brought your horse around and made indiscreet inquiries after you both, I feared that some evil would befall you before I saw you again. Sit, please, and tell us all that passed."

Miss Landry asked, "Father, may I first get us a little food to break our fast? We have had aught but some ramp I was able to gather in the woods."

Her father said, "Of course, I should have thought of it myself." When he saw her wince at stepping toward the larder, though, he said "Nay, stop, sit down and take off your boots, child. What have you done to yourself?"

Although Alec looked away delicately as the girl's boots and then stockings came off, he couldn't help but glance over at hearing both his father and hers exclaim as her feet were bared, exposing blisters that had ruptured and torn, leaving open sores across her heels and the tops of both feet. The side of one foot was rubbed raw, as well, and Alec stood to wave both men away.

"I've seen worse," he said, kneeling before her chair and taking her feet in his hands, turning them one way and the other to be sure that he had the full measure of her injuries. Miss Landry sat passively, although he could have sworn that a small smile lifted the edges of her mouth as he turned to Mister Landry to ask, "Have you clean bandages and perhaps a little rum?"

Her father nodded and hurried off.

To Miss Landry, Alec said, "The rum is for you, as this is liable to hurt quite a bit, and it will also reduce the inflammation so that you can resume your daily activities without delay."

She said faintly, "They were giving me pain, but I did not anticipate they were in such a state."

He scoffed in reply, "Nay, 'tis not so bad as that. I spoke the truth when I said I've seen worse, and what's more, with some proper care, those afflicted were back on the march the next day."

What he didn't say was that some of those same men had fallen prey to infections and worse for not having been able to stay in one place until they healed.

His father shot him a questioning look, and he nodded back with what he hoped was a reassuring confidence. "Father, I was not trained to physic the men's hurts, but I saw it done enough that I would have to be a blockhead to not have learned the general principles."

"Carry on, then, son," his father said, and Alec thought he detected a note of new respect in his voice. "I should not have supposed that you were inclined toward the healing arts, but 'tis a good thing, apparently, that you are."

Mister Landry returned with a shirt and a bottle, and immediately started ripping strips from the bottom of the shirt. In reply to Alec's glance, he said, "'Tis clean, and I've less need of it than does my daughter."

Alec nodded. "A tot of the rum for your daughter then, and one for yourself as well, if you think it will trouble you to see her hurt."

Miss Landry gulped visibly, and her father handed her the bottle without comment. She took a healthy swig from it, and handed the bottle back to him, coughing and gasping at the burn of the liquor.

Alec took advantage of her distraction to puncture the largest of the unruptured blisters, pinching it between his fingernails, and squeezing out the clear liquid with a quick, gentle touch.

She cried out, and Alec saw her father lift the bottle to his own lips.

"Sorry, Miss Landry. I do not seek to hurt you, but only to release the overabundance of whatever humors fill your blisters." He shook his head ruefully, looking back toward his father. "I did not advance my education in healing so far as to fully comprehend the reasons for the things that the physics did to help with our hurts."

As he tended to Miss Landry's blisters, Alec could not help but notice that her feet were small and delicate in comparison with his own, and that the veins across their tops made a branching, lovely tracery where they were not concealed by blisters.

Although he tried not to take note of her finely-formed ankles, never mind the graceful curve of her legs as they disappeared under her skirts, he found it hard to concentrate on the treatment at hand, and it was with some degree of both reluctance and relief that he accepted the strips of cloth from her father with which to bandage her wounds.

When he was done, he could see that Miss Landry's eyes

were bright with unshed tears at the pain he'd inflicted in the course of trying to physic her to the best of his knowledge.

Without thinking, he took her hand and brushed a kiss against the back of it, murmuring, "I am sincerely sorry for your hurt, Miss Landry."

Her eyes widened, but she nodded, replying softly, "I know that you do only what is necessary to see to my health, Alec."

Both his father and hers seemed even more surprised at his action than was she, and he saw them exchange a significant glance.

He sighed inwardly, knowing that they attached more meaning to the momentary intimacy than he had ever intended.

Or, he wondered, had he perhaps intended it?

He sighed again, wishing that his own thoughts were clearer to him. He stood and resumed his seat at the table.

Mister Landry sprang to his feet, saying, "Since Holly is indisposed, I shall go and fetch something for you both to eat, while you tell us of your escape and your travels here."

Alec's father spoke up while Mister Landry busied himself gathering a plate of bread and cheese, and a couple of mugs of cider to set before them.

"The jailer said that you took part in the murder of his successor as the chief of the guard there."

Alec shook his head. "Nay, I did no such thing, though I did participate in the ruse that permitted his killer to seize him."

He frowned.

Alec ignored that. "You said that the jailer's name was Garrick? Was his given name Jonas, by some chance?"

His father nodded. "Aye, I do believe that he introduced himself by that name. 'Twas the man who arranged my visits and aided you with your letters to me, I believe, though I never much marked him in our previous meetings."

Alec said, "That's the man, yes. He was displaced by Gad over an ill-considered scheme to effect an escape before the one that just... happened."

He described how Charles had seen, and taken, the opportunity offered by Miss Landry's visit, and the events of their flight from the prison.

He gave Holly a look of open admiration as he said, "Once we were outside of the prison walls, though, it was Miss Landry who conceived how we might find refuge under your roof, and who helped me find the way here, despite us needing to stay away from familiar roads and make the trip entirely under our own power."

Holly blushed faintly, saying, "Nay, we should never have found our way were it not for Mister Tinsworth's knowledge of the movement of the heavens and the means of evading a hunt."

She quickly filled in the details of his navigation by the position of the sun, and his use of the stone fence to hide their tracks.

Alec's father said quietly, "And yet, Jonas needed no tracks to look for us here. I presume that he or someone else will return once you have not been found for a few days. New-Gate may not keep its prisoners very well, but its jailers are determined to return them to its crypts, rather than let them range over the countryside."

Mister Landry said soberly, "There is no safe place for us here, while the rebels yet hold sway over Connecticut. If we can arrange passage to New-York, however, where the British regulars are in control, we can await the end of this accursed war there in some security."

Alec's father said, "'Tis a fine idea, but there are almost one hundred and fifty miles of road between here and there, and most of that is held by unfriendly forces, who will be alert for any unusual travelers."

Miss Landry spoke up then, her eyes dancing with some private amusement. "I have an idea," she said, "but I don't think Alec will much like it."

Chapter 23

Alec sighed. He supposed that he would have to become accustomed to Miss Landry being right about things.

No, he corrected himself, he must think of her as Missus Harrison.

He scratched his head where the borrowed wig sat atop his newly close-shorn scalp, making him itch something fierce. And, he reminded himself, he must think of himself as Mister Harrison.

He and Miss Landry — easiest just to think of her as Holly, he decided — sat in the back seat of her father's Jersey wagon, shielded by both changed appearances and the cloth-covered top. Their fathers rode in the front seat, chatting amiably and giving every appearance of normality to anyone who they might pass. The horses were in fine spirits, and they had long since left the immediate precincts of the Landry home.

Alec had to admit that Holly's idea was ingenious, as much as it seemed to be making certain assumptions about his plans.

She'd started by sitting him down in the barn and giving him a good, close shave. She'd followed that with a close crop of his hair, and then fitted a wig borrowed from her father.

Together with a proper suit of clothing borrowed from his own father, Alec felt like a new man, and when he'd looked in the glass, he barely recognized himself. The hope was that anyone looking for him would likewise fail to see the escaped prisoner, and would instead see the newlywed gentleman, off to New-York to present his bride to family in the city.

Holly pulled their blanket close around them against the chill of the approaching dusk, and Alec heard his father remark to Mister Landry that they had best be looking for a public house in which to get some rooms. He felt Holly's head droop onto his shoulder, and his arm went around her quite naturally and comfortably.

Once again, he found himself falling asleep wondering at the sweetness of her hair in his nose.

He awoke as the gentle rocking of the wagon in motion came to a stop.

Mister Landry called out to someone, "Do you know if there are rooms available within?"

A polite voice answered, "Aye, not much in the way of travelers these days, as you likely know. Shall I stable your horses for you and call a boy to fetch your bags?"

"That would be quite kind of you, yes." He leaned in to face Holly and Alec. "Come on out, my dears. I shall arrange a room for you."

Alec froze for a moment. A room, that was to say a shared room?

On reflection, it would be surpassingly odd for newlyweds to do otherwise, but... a room?

Shaking off the thought for the time being, he stepped down and turned to extend a hand to Holly.

She smiled at him, as though sensing his discomfort, and again he was amazed at the transformation a smile brought to her face. She stepped down and caught him gazing at her. As the stable boy led the wagon away, she asked quietly, "What is it, Alec?"

He shook himself out of the reverie he'd fallen into, and said just as quietly, "Naught of import, Holly. Just wonder at the fact that you were so immediately ready to dedicate yourself to ensuring my escape from those who pursue me, that you were willing to assume this role, even for the sake of a ruse. It's more than I could ask of a friend."

She smiled again, this time with open gaiety. "'Tis no less than I could do for a true friend, Alec." She lowered her eyes and added delicately, "And I find that I hope it may one day be more than a mere role for a ruse."

Alec's eyes widened as her meaning struck him. He answered without being aware of having given the matter conscious consideration, his voice low and sincere.

"I find that I should like that very much."

Their fathers stood looking on, bemused, as Holly threw herself into Alec's arms, and the couple embraced in a very convincing demonstration of newly-wed affection.

Mister Landry gave Alec's father a significant look, and motioned for the door of the public house, saying, "Let us see to those rooms, and leave these two to themselves, shall we?"

They were still comfortably in each other's arms when Mister Landry came back out. "I've a room for you, where it may be more comfortable to continue your conversation."

They disentangled themselves, and Mister Landry led them inside, where the innkeeper touched his knuckle to his forehead in a sort of salute. He conducted them to their chamber, a smallish room with a single narrow bed. Without comment, he held the door open for them to enter, and then closed it behind them quietly.

Alec gently smiled down at Holly. "I suppose we'll have to each admit that our fathers knew what was best for us, despite any resistance we might have felt."

She gave him a sardonic look. "You may have felt resistance — though on what account, I cannot conceive — but I was merely hopeful not be married off to a man who resided several times the depth of a grave under the earth, and whose most likely prospect was to move up to a proper grave in due time."

Her smile returned fully as she added, "Now that you reside on the surface again, I have no remaining resistance to my father's wishes, and it brings me a heart full of joy to hear you say that you have overcome whatever cause prevented you from giving your father's wishes full consideration before now."

He pondered his words for a moment, hoping that he would never in the years ahead give voice to his other reservations in any way whatever, and answered, "In truth, my resistance sprang from much the same source, as well as wanting to have the chance to come to know your qualities more fully for myself, rather than depending upon someone else's judgment. Though I trust that my father means well, I must discover my own mind on some matters, mustn't I?"

"And have you discovered your own mind in this matter?"

"Aye, I believe I have." Alec took a deep breath. "You are both more resourceful and more capable than I ever hoped to find you. When you would have been fully justified in parting ways with me and leaving me to devise my own escape, you instead threw your lot in with mine and helped me find my way to safety."

He gestured at the wig on his head. "Having recovered the comfort of your own roof and the company of your own father, instead of sending me off with my father to find some means of ensuring our security, you concocted this fantastic scheme."

Glancing around the room, he added, "Even knowing that should our scheme be discovered, you would not only face charges for assisting a fugitive, but also suffer irreparable harm to your reputation, you have not hesitated."

Shrugging, she said, "As I said before, I have only sought to be a true friend, in a moment when you seemed most in need of one."

Glancing at the bed, she smiled. "As for my reputation, if you are concerned for it, you may sleep on the floor if you insist, but for my part, I should prefer to share the warmth of the bed, even though we remain clothed."

She smiled directly at him now. "Until I shall leave behind the name 'Harrison' and assume a different one, that is."

Alec could feel his face turn hot, all the way to the tips of his ears, and her giggle at his reaction seemed to release something within him, and he joined her in helpless, hooting laughter. He laughed at their discomfort, the absurdity of the situation, and eventually, at the suppressed shock and joy at being free of captivity.

He clutched at her arm for support, and sank to the floor with her as his chortling renewed her own, and they both were overcome with mirth, passing the waves of guffaws back and forth as though they were a thing passing between their hands.

Finally, they both regained some measure of control over themselves, and they each practiced taking deep breaths, their chuckles slowing to no more than occasional outbursts of giggles.

Holly was the first to regain the power of speech. "I—What was that about, Alec? I have never been so affected in any moment before this one."

He shook his head, tears streaming down his face, and pulled her into a seated embrace, past caring about how awkward it might be. "I am simply overcome with gratitude, for being alive and restored to liberty, for your friendship, and for the simple company of your presence. I am convinced that it is not our fathers who brought us together, but some divine providence, so perfect are we for one another. You see that within me which is ridiculous, and aren't afraid to show it to me, though you don't heap ridicule upon me, but help me to overcome it."

He released her and looked at her, his expression filled with admiration. "You perceive the heart of matters in an instant, and while others — including myself — are still trying to identify the outlines of our predicament, you're already busy solving the problem."

Looking at her face, still shining with the exertion of their bout of shared laughter, he wondered how he could ever have thought her plain. Her eyes sparkled with lively intelligence and good humor, and the smile that touched her lips gave the sense that she might at any moment burst out in fresh hilarity again.

She held his gaze for a long moment. "I, too, could be convinced that whatever our fathers saw in proposing a partnership between us was some sort of inspiration. Your qualities, beyond the mere perseverance to have survived in brutal captivity, seem perfectly suited to serve as a foil to my shortcomings."

He began to scoff, but she held up a hand. "I am only too sensible of my frailties. When I succumbed to hopelessness at the stone fence, you did not leave me there to ensure your escape, but came back for me immediately, and made me feel safe and comforted enough to fall asleep, and even sleep soundly in the midst of the wilds, a thing I would never have thought possible for me."

She smiled, her eyes going distant with memory. "And when I shaved you that first time, drawing blood, rather than becoming angry, you turned the other cheek, just exactly as Christ commands us to do. And after I'd cut your hair, I could not resist the temptation to suggest that you were no gentleman, and rather than rising to my barb, you swallowed your pride."

Her eyes returned to his and crinkled in a deep grin. "And here you are, a true gentleman, in any sense of the word I could name, having served your King and country, having saved the girl in distress, and dressed in proper fashion as befits your station in life."

He shook his head, smiling, and stood, brushing the dust from the floor off of his trousers. "I thank you for the reminder that these clothes are but borrowed, and I ought care for them better." He extended a hand down to her. "Come, let us go and see what sustenance the innkeeper is offering with our room."

Down in the dining room, they were just taking their seats when a bored-looking man entered and handed over a paper to the innkeeper before ambling back out again.

The innkeeper looked over the paper grimly, and then turned and pushed it over a nail on the wall behind him, covering a stack of similar-looking pages.

Alec gave Holly a quizzical look and murmured, "I don't have my letters. What does it say?"

She frowned, muttering, "We shall have to see about that, my friend," and turned to look at the paper — along with several other people in the tavern, Alec noticed.

After a moment, she grinned merrily, and said, "Well, it seems that there has been a prison-break from the New-Gate, if you can imagine such a thing, and a handful of prisoners yet remain at liberty. One shares your given name — what a funny coincidence that is, though his surname is different! — and is described as being a danger to all true patriots, having killed both a guard and a prisoner in the course of his escape."

Her eyes wide in a very convincing act at playing the role she had set out for herself in their scheme, she commented, "We shall have to be alert to the possibility that we may encounter this ruffian along our way. He sounds very dangerous, but I trust that you and our fathers will keep me safe from any hazard he might present."

She grasped his upper arm and smiled girlishly at him, but he could feel her willing her strength into his spirit through her hand. All he had to do, he knew, was to follow her lead, and they would be safe all the way to New-York City.

He smiled back at her and said, "You may rely on me completely, my dear friend."

Chapter 24

Back in the wagon, Holly's comforting warmth pressed against his side, Alec was lost in thought, looking out over the passing countryside, when he felt Holly stiffen suddenly beside him. Following her gaze to the road ahead, he saw a clump of men gathered by the road, wearing the uniforms of some rebel unit or another. The soldiers moved about a farm wagon that had preceded them on the road for most of the day, evidently inspecting its contents and passengers.

Mister Landry turned briefly in his seat, making eye contact with both Holly and Alec, giving them a small, tight smile. "Not to worry, Mister and Missus Harrison. Just a routine checkpoint, looking for smuggled goods."

He turned forward, saying to Alec's father, "Probably should have thought to smuggle something, as it would likely have been most welcome in the city."

Mister Tinsworth snorted, but said nothing.

Mister Landry guided his wagon to a stop behind the first one, and Alec concentrated on ensuring that his expression was merely bored, and on keeping the fear that crept up the back of his throat off of his face.

Under the blanket, Holly's hand moved to hold his, and he returned her grip with gratitude.

A soldier stepped away from the wagon in front of theirs

and approached. "What business have you on this route?" The man's words were spoken in a tone that suggested he'd said them a thousand times already.

Mister Landry answered, gesturing at Holly and Alec. "We hope to go to the city, to present my new son-in-law to my family there."

The soldier's glance slid over Alec without slowing, paused at Holly's form, and then returned to her father's face. "Tories?" His voice was sharp and disapproving.

Mister Tinsworth sighed and said, "We have tried to stay out of this whole affair, but yes, my family in the city are Tories, else I'd have had them out to my home instead."

The soldier nodded. "Better for them to stay there, where they experience the discomfort of the British occupation directly, than to venture out into the countryside and sow trouble."

Alec's father spoke up now. "Is it truly so bad in the city? If so, it might be better for us to turn back, rather than risk the safety of the newly-married couple."

Mister Landry shook his head dismissively. "Nay, Phillip, my family has written to me and they say that it is overcrowded, but the regulars patrol the streets and keep good order, even if they are sometimes overly harsh."

The soldier nodded. "That comports well with the reports I have heard from travelers passing out of the city. Some goods are dear, of course, but 'Tis said that they get regular supply from the Indies, from Halifax, and even from London."

He glanced down at the men's feet. "I'll need to look through your effects before I can permit you to pass, of course. All manner of contraband is being smuggled into the city, and we are doing our level best to avoid allowing disloyal people from supplying succor to the occupiers."

"Of course," Mister Landry said.

The soldier opened each of their traveling valises, glanced through them, and closed them back up. "Wait here," he said. "I will have my commanding officer write out a passport for you that will enable you to travel through the rest of this country without further difficulty. Once you reach the British line, they will, naturally, want to examine you themselves, but your errand is ordinary enough. May I have your names?"

Mister Landry bowed slightly in his seat and gave all four names, smoothly pronouncing Alec and Holly as the Harrisons.

The soldier said, "I shall return as quickly as I can."

"Your servant, sir," Mister Landry replied, and settled back to wait.

In front of them, the soldiers appeared to be completely unloading the other wagon, setting barrels into the mud, over the objections of the drover, and even prying a couple of the barrels open. Alec saw one of the soldiers step back abruptly, dropping the lid back onto the small barrel he'd just opened.

The other soldiers started laughing and hooting, and Alec could hear the one who'd reacted say, "I've never witnessed potted eels that badly gone off before, and I hope never to again."

The drover looked angry at the fun that the soldiers were making of his cargo, and Alec felt bad for the man. He was doubtless just trying to sell his wares, and had hoped to pass through the checkpoint without unnecessary difficulty.

The breeze shifted then, and with it, so did Alec's sympathies. What kind of devil would carry something that smelled so foul, anywhere, for any purpose?

Beside him, Holly's face had gone pale, and both Mister Landry and Alec's father had covered their noses and mouths in reaction to the overpowering stench of dead fish that enveloped them. Even the horses shifted uncomfortably in their harnesses.

The soldier who'd inspected their wagon was speaking to man sitting at a spindly portable desk of some sort. The officer glanced back at their wagon, chuckled to see their reactions to the smell from the first wagon, and produced a printed sheet from within the desk. He dipped his pen and scratched in a few words.

He handed the soldier the paper and waved dismissively at their wagon. The soldier waved Mister Landry forward, and as their wagon maneuvered around the barrels on the road, he handed the paper over to Mister Landry. The eel smell was less here, and Alec gratefully breathed deeply of the fresher air.

"A pleasant trip to you, sir, and congratulations to you two," he said, catching Alec and Holly's eyes.

Her voice clear and pleasant, Holly said, "Thank you, kind sir, and I hope that your duty is pleasant and without further such hazards."

The soldier chuckled and motioned them on down the road.

As they bumped over the uneven ground to the side of the road, and then back onto the main road, Alec could feel Holly slump beside him.

"Thank heavens for that poor farmer and his miserable eels," she said. "Without that smell, we might have been there for hours."

The remainder of the trip was relatively easy. A desultory

guard in a crimson jacket gave their pass a quick examination at the verge of the city, and in short order, their horses were clopping on the cobbles as they passed between buildings of three, four, and even five stories, until they followed the directions of a passing boy to a public house with rooms available.

It was only then that Alec knew he had finally escaped.

Chapter 25

The city was dirty, unbelievably overcrowded, and loud at all hours of the day and night. It was almost enough to make Alec miss the comparative peace and quiet of the mine.

Almost, but not quite.

Although the need to maintain the ruse had passed now that they were in a place under friendly management, he and Holly had continued to pass time together, and the lack of available space in any tavern in the city required them to continue sharing a room.

Although Alec's sense of propriety was strained by the arrangement, he could not deny that their time together was an exceedingly pleasant necessity. They had fallen into a routine of walking together in the mornings, after breaking their fast with Mister Landry and Alec's father, and then in the afternoon, joining Mister Landry as he entertained callers of all sorts.

"I've so many correspondents here in the city," he explained to Alec one morning over a meal taken in the tavern dining room. "Men I've known as acquaintances and friends, and men with whom I've conducted business for years. My presence now in the very heart of the city comes as something of a miracle to their minds, as they'd considered it likely that I should be seized up by our restive American cousins, or at the least, dispossessed of my holdings by force."

He chuckled ruefully. "I have now been dispossessed, but it was I who abandoned my property. It was, of course, in service of the safety of you and my daughter, but the rebels cannot have failed to take advantage of my absence."

"Will you not be able to reclaim your property, once their General Washington is defeated, and their Congress is in chains on the way to trial in London?" Alec had heard rumors around the city that gave him a good sense of confidence that these satisfying events might be reported with any day's post.

Mister Landry smiled sadly at him. "It will not likely be so easy, dear boy. Once somebody else has established housekeeping in my own home, and has set his horses to graze my former paddocks, it is a difficult matter indeed. You may have heard it said that possession is eleven points in the law, and there are but twelve to be considered." He laughed bitterly. "Of course, if the terms of the rebel surrender are clear enough, that last point may be sufficient."

Holly, who'd been following the conversation with lively interest, but remaining uncharacteristically quiet up to this point, now spoke up. "No matter what the terms of the surrender might be, I think that I'll have a hard time living amongst people who would seize our property over a difference in policy, never mind imprisoning Alec and his fellow militiamen in conditions of utter barbarity."

Alec smiled at her, and rested his hand atop hers. He glanced at his father, and then addressed Mister Landry, "My father mentioned that you and Holly have some prospects in England worth consideration, as well?"

His father gave Alec a shrewd look, then smiled and looked away.

Mister Landry answered, "Aye, so I did," he said sadly. "But England is no place for a man who's grown accustomed to being able to spread his arms without knocking into his neighbor's shoulder."

Mister Landry snorted and glanced around. "Of course, this city is far worse even than the English countryside."

Alec nodded. "I can scarcely sleep for the movement of carts and wagons at all hours of the night, and the drill of troops is liable to disturb one just as they've finally reached sleep."

His father said, "One does grow used to it with time. I spent a year in London at about your age, and while it took a while, I did learn to dismiss the sounds of people around me there, so that I could sleep soundly regardless. Indeed, after I came to live in the countryside, I had to learn to sleep in quiet all over again."

"'Tis a curious thing," Mister Landry agreed. "Of course, you can hardly have been accustomed to complete silence in prison, being held in such proximity to so many other men."

"Oh, aye, they were nothing like quiet, particularly at night. Of course, we were all weary to the bone most nights, from one sort of labor or another, so it hardly ever happened that we had any difficulty sleeping, no matter what went on around us."

Holly spoke up again. "I've hardly noticed the noise from without, as once Alec passes into sleep at night, there is so much noise from within the room. It may be that he was not disturbed by the snores of the other prisoners only because his own snoring was so loud."

Alec's father guffawed, grinning at his son. "You'll not find that easy to refute, my boy, as it will require both that you stay awake longer than she, and that you discover that she is your equal or better."

Alec returned his father's smile. "I have no difficulty acknowledging that Miss Landry is likely my equal or better in this, as in so many other things."

Holly gave both men a fierce simulation of a glare. "You'll not trap me into a declaration of my superiority in the matter of snoring by false flattery in other matters. 'Tis a brigand's strategy, and I'd thought you more honest than that."

Alec gave her a playful smirk. "But, Holly, I recall that just yesterday you were holding forth on the necessity of giving women their due in all matters. We are but observing that convention to the very letter, don't you see?"

"Oh, you'll give me your due," she growled, but under her mock anger, there was a note of cheerful confidence in his friendship and respect.

Alec noticed it, and smiled at her even more widely. "Gladly, dear friend. Gladly."

A man burst through the tavern door and conferred quickly with the innkeeper. Mister Landry took note of the disturbance, and after the visitor left, he called out to the innkeeper, "What seems to be the matter, good sir?"

The innkeeper waved a hand at the door dismissively. "Oh, he's spreading rumors about General Washington's movements. It seems that some force of men was spotted this morning at Manhattan."

Alec froze, and then asked urgently, "On Manhattan itself?"

"Nay, on the overlook from the New-Jersey side. That fellow says he slipped away before our forces could address him properly. By the time our boys had his range and might have been able to engage him with cannon, he had gone." The innkeeper shrugged. "It's always the same story with this Washington. He is not shy of a proper fight, and yet our men always seem to be just barely unable to engage him when they discover him."

Alec pursed his lips. "I've heard much the same." He felt a wave of relief wash over him, though, as he'd known that if Washington were entrapped, and there was any chance at all that his service might help to finish the job, he would have felt obligated to seek out the nearest militia and put himself at the disposal of its officers.

He glanced over at Holly, who seemed to have divined his thoughts, as though she had a spy reporting intelligence from the very seat of his mind. She was frowning, but there was an air of resignation in it, too. In any event, he was glad that the issue would remain theoretical only.

Alec's father seemed to have picked up on Alec's thoughts, as well. "Our families have done their part in this war, Alec," he said quietly. "I have sacrificed two sons entirely, lost my helpmeet, and have seen my last son locked in a hole in the ground in defense of the Crown. Let someone else have the chance to do their part, and take their turn with the hangman's noose about their shoulders, ready to jerk taut at any moment."

Alec's mouth pressed into a tight line for a long moment, and he glanced from his father's eyes, weary and defeated, to Holly's, steadfast but guarded.

He lowered his chin. "It makes the incomplete discharge of my duty seem like an unfulfilled poverty, but I know also that those who serve under arms do not serve alone, and indeed, I am come to understand that we who have carried a gun have borne only a fraction of the load of this war."

Looking at each of the members of his family — for he realized with a burst of love for each of them that they were all his family — Alec said quietly, "Those who wait by the doors of their homes for word from a distant pen, those who fret by a fire, making clothes for limbs that may no longer need them, and those who see their life's work drain away under forces beyond their control, you all serve as surely as the soldier."

He took a deep breath. "I'll not ask any of us to serve any longer. We have, each of us, served well and faithfully. You are correct, Father, that it is time for me to let go of the vanity that I alone must take up this duty."

Looking into Holly's eyes steadily now, he said, "I have more important duties to attend to now, and it is time that I stop evading them."

Chapter 26

Alec stood beside Holly, squinting into the sunrise at the railing of a ship, passing out of New-York harbor, bound for Bristol. He glanced behind him to the city that had been home for the better part of a year, its close-packed buildings dwindling in the distance. Their fathers stood speaking tensely along the rail, discussing the business implications of the fall of Cornwallis' forces in Virginia.

The practical result of that stunning defeat — it was said that the French had finally avenged themselves at Yorktown for the loss of Quebec — was that Alec and Mister Landry had simultaneously decided that it was past time to collect Holly's dowry from her uncle.

Mister Landry had booked passage for all four of them on the next ship he could find, and they had closed up their rooms at the public house. Alec felt a pang at leaving the place that had seen the first months of his marriage to Holly, but there was no sadness in seizing the future that awaited them.

He slipped his arm around Holly's waist, and she leaned into him, her hair tickling his nose and smelling still of sunshine.

Also in Audiobook

Many readers love the experience of turning the pages in a paper book such as the one you hold in your hands. Others enjoy hearing a skilled narrator tell them a story, bringing the words on the page to life.

Brief Candle Press has arranged to have *The Mine* produced as a high-quality audiobook, and you can listen to a sample and learn where to purchase it in that form by scanning the QR code below with your phone, tablet, or other device, or going to the Web address shown.

Happy listening!

bit.ly/TheMineAudio

Historical Notes

Writing about the experience of prisoners of war during the American Revolution was a challenging decision for me, as I had previously done little research into the psychology and daily experience of imprisonment. I've come across passing mentions in the literature about the terrible conditions under which American captives were held on prison hulks in New-York harbor, but that story is one for another time, perhaps.

The history of the New-Gate Prison in Connecticut gave me an opportunity to approach some of the interesting questions of the prisoner-of-war experience in the Revolution within a slightly more contained environment, and so it made for a story that I thought I could do justice.

While I've no direct evidence of the sort of brutality I depict being inflicted on prisoners at the New-Gate Prison actually happening there, feelings ran high enough during the Revolution that I have little trouble envisioning such events taking place, whether at the hands of the guards or of the other prisoners.

Gad Sheldon was a real guard at New-Gate, and was actually killed in the 1781 breakout, though the records I could find did not record the exact manner of his death, which left me some latitude for the story. I have opted to depict him as a cruel and brutal jailer, and if I have erred in taking this liberty with his character, I do hope that any who might have a stake in his reputation will forgive me the literary license I have taken.

The greatest liberty I've taken with history, though, is my depiction of the employment of the prisoners at the New-Gate Gaol in 1781. In fact, the nail-making industry was not established there for another nine years, and at the time when the Revolution was still underway, as far as I can tell, the prisoners were simply stuffed underground and left there to survive on what food was sent down to them, supported by the efforts of their families, with no employment whatever.

However, that would have made for a much more dull and claustrophobic story, so I opted to pull part of the New-Gate story forward by a few years for my dramatic purposes. I do hope that readers and historians will forgive me the small violence I've done to the facts in the service of telling what I hope is a more compelling story of an almost entirely neglected aspect of the Revolutionary War.

Acknowledgements

As always, I must acknowledge the legions of researchers who've written over the past centuries about so many of the aspects of the American Revolution that make it into my stories. The fact that this wealth of data, interpretation, and knowledge are all available at our fingertips represents the single most important factor in my ability to spin a richly-textured tale, with some confidence that it reflects the experience of people who lived through that tumultuous era.

After I drafted this story, I reached out to the fine people at the State of Connecticut who have recently undertaken the project of making the Old New-Gate site accessible to the public. Their enthusiasm for my project, and their support of my work on it, have been deeply gratifying. Morgan Bengel's comments on the draft were particularly helpful, and I am pleased to be able to acknowledge her kind assistance.

My editor, Jen McDonnell, supplied me with invaluable feedback and corrections in the last stages of this book's development. Whatever errors may have survived her eagle eye, though, are entirely of my own creation.

Thank You

I deeply appreciate you spending the past couple of hundred pages with the characters and events of a world long past, yet hopefully relevant today.

If you enjoyed this book, I'd also be grateful for a kind review on your favorite bookseller's Web site or social media outlet. Word of mouth is the best way to make me successful, so that I can bring you even more high-quality stories of bygone times.

I'd love to hear directly from you, too—feel free to reach out to me via my Facebook page, Twitter feed, or Web site and let me know what you liked, and what you would like me to work on more.

Again, thank you for reading, for telling your friends about this book, for giving it as a gift or dropping off a copy in your favorite classroom or library. With your support and encouragement, we'll find even more times and places to explore together.

larsdhhedbor.com
Facebook: Lars.D.H.Hedbor
@LarsDHHedbor on Twitter

Enjoy a preview of the next book in the
Tales From a Revolution series:

<u>The Siege</u>

Nathaniel Wooster never saw which of the advancing redcoats fired the shot that struck him. The line of enemy horsemen had come close enough to have become individual men—with distinct features, expressions, and even voices—before his commander had given the shouted order to fire.

Just after his musket had roared in his ear and had kicked back into his shoulder, Nathaniel felt as though he'd been punched hard on the arm that supported the wooden stock. The sensation honestly confused him at first, until he realized that his hand would no longer hold the weight of his weapon. He watched the precious musket tumble away from a useless arm even as his knees began to feel weak.

Before he'd even had time to register the pain of the wound, however, the British line was on them, sabers flashing among the hapless American militiamen. Though they'd been drilled and trained to regard themselves as soldiers, most of them were hardly more than farmers or tradesmen, and none of them had any sense of how to defend themselves against a yard of brilliant biting steel descending to slice and tear flesh.

As he collapsed to the ground, his musket forgotten as it dropped from his insensate hand, Nathaniel had just enough presence of mind to see that he was one of the lucky ones. The man who'd formed up to his left lay on his back, eyes unblinking to the sky, his neck sliced deeply enough that Nathaniel could see the white of bone inside the sagging wound. The man on his right was moaning and clutching at his belly, where the passage of a British saber had sliced through cloth, skin, and guts with equal indifference. Though Nathaniel had seen little action before now, he had no doubt that this would be that man's last day on Earth.

The redcoat footsoldiers who'd followed the cavalry charge were now pushing and shoving amongst the few Americans who still stood, using their muskets as clubs, and the horsemen wheeled about through the massed Americans, swinging their now-befouled sabers in clear menace as they strove with their enemies. Nathaniel heard a grunt behind him, and a British soldier fell facing him, clutching at his chest. The man's eyes locked onto his, and for the space of a few lazy heartbeats—heard as a rush in Nathaniel's ears, and seen as a surge of blood between the other man's fingers—they stared at each other.

Then the other man's eyes rolled back into his head, and he was still, aside from the steady trickle of blood into the bare earth beneath him. Soon enough, even that had ceased, and Nathaniel willed himself to look away.

After what seemed like an eternity of slowing, sporadic gunfire in the distance and the screams and moans of men nearby and further strewn about the field, Nathaniel heard the cry passed from voice to voice. "Quarter! They've asked for quarter! The day is ours!"

As he focused on his labored breathing, Nathaniel wondered whether the white flag would be honored this time, or whether someone would again violate it and precipitate another round of senseless violence. His thoughts were tending to wander now, though, and he could not seem to hold onto a single thread for very long.

He found himself wondering whether he would see his Ma again, or watch another sunrise from the top of the bluff back home. He had paused in his morning chores often enough to enjoy the sight that it was graven in his mind. The purpling horizon gave way to deeper reds than even that which had seeped through his enemy's fingers, finally punctuated by a sudden gasp of brilliant sunlight as the day began.

He found himself wondering how this day would end. Would he sink into a grateful slumber, or would he find a more lengthy rest in an anonymous grave, accompanied by friends and enemies alike? Would he be reunited with his brother, who had been carried off by the pox so many years before, and would they again play their favorite games with hoop and stick?

Or would he lay here in this field of carnage, drifting in and out of the world of pain and fear, unrelieved by any sleep, whether eternal or just an ordinary night? His stomach lurched at the thought of his Ma wondering for month after month about his fate, or worse yet, receiving positive word by an impersonal post that her only remaining son would never return.

He was just picturing this dismal possibility in cruel detail when he heard a squad moving over the field, and a voice calling out, "Here's one that's still breathing, lieutenant." A boot appeared before his eyes, and Nathaniel wondered at it, struck by the lack of splashed grime on its well-blacked, supple leather.

The man bent and not ungently rolled Nathaniel over to lie on his back. The movement sparked agonies in Nathaniel's arm, and he cried out as the world closed in around him in gathering darkness. He could see, though, that the man's elegantly-appointed jacket was crimson, and his expression disdainful.

"Bring a litter over here. Our orders are to treat all wounded, regardless of whether they be ours or the rebels."

Look for The Siege: Tales From a Revolution - Virginia _at your favorite booksellers._